"You!"

Dray Carlisle reached to switch on a bedside lamp.

"Yes," she confirmed as light filled the darkness. "Me."

"I don't believe it. What are you doing here?"

"Right at the moment, trying to get Ellie back to sleep," she responded as the baby's cries escalated. "Unless you'd like to do it? In which case, could I suggest a slightly less aggressive tone?"

She offered the baby to him, but it was purely a mocking gesture.

His eyes bored into her as he responded, "Very funny…I'll wait outside."

"If that's what you want." Cass's tone was dismissive.

"No, what I *want*," he growled back, "is to go to bed."

Cass shrugged. She wasn't stopping him.

"Don't worry, that wasn't a proposition."

"I wasn't worried," she returned sharply.

It backfired, however, as he paused briefly to murmur, "Now, that *is* interesting."

ALISON FRASER was born and brought up in the far north of Scotland. She studied English literature at university and taught math for a while, then became a computer programmer. She took up writing as a hobby and it is still very much so, in that she doesn't take it too seriously! Alison currently lives with her husband, children and dogs in Birmingham, England, and is in her forties—she doesn't know what she wants to be when she grows up!

Books by Alison Fraser

HARLEQUIN PRESENTS®
2149—BRIDE REQUIRED

Alison Fraser

HER SISTER'S BABY

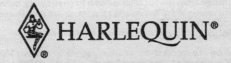

HARLEQUIN®

TORONTO • NEW YORK • LONDON
AMSTERDAM • PARIS • SYDNEY • HAMBURG
STOCKHOLM • ATHENS • TOKYO • MILAN • MADRID
PRAGUE • WARSAW • BUDAPEST • AUCKLAND

ISBN 0-373-12190-3

HER SISTER'S BABY

First North American Publication 2001.

Copyright © 2000 by Alison Fraser.

This edition published by arrangement with Harlequin Books S.A.

® and TM are trademarks of the publisher. Trademarks indicated with
® are registered in the United States Patent and Trademark Office, the
Canadian Trade Marks Office and in other countries.

Visit us at www.eHarlequin.com

Printed in U.S.A.

CHAPTER ONE

CASS walked from the tube station with her eyes down. It was well after dark and, though the streets were lit, few people were about in the driving early summer rain. She had no umbrella, her suede jacket was becoming quickly sodden and her hair hung like rat-tails round her face.

It was times like these she wished she had a car to service instead of a student bank loan. She was just too tired to run. She'd worked the entire weekend and longed for her own bed and eight hours' uninterrupted sleep.

When she turned into her home street, she was in no state to notice anything, even the sleek expensive car that didn't quite belong in her neighbourhood. She sailed past it, thinking only of getting the key in her door and reaching shelter.

The driver noticed her, however. He'd been there over an hour and he wasn't a man used to waiting. Impatience had sharpened his powers of observation and he was out of the car before she'd reached her gate. He followed quickly, having an idea she would close the door on him if she were given the chance.

Cass heard the footsteps behind her and felt the unease most women had on a dark night. She rifled in her bag as she walked and had her key ready by the time she reached her front step.

The echo of footsteps stopped at her gate and made her fingers clumsy as she tried to fit the Yale in the lock and dropped it instead. Unease became alarm as she turned, prepared to cry out at the dark-coated figure bearing down on her.

'Don't panic,' a deep, dry voice told her. 'It's me.'

For a moment Cass didn't recognise the voice—or him—then her nerves steadied and she realised who it was.

'Drayton Carlisle,' he added, as if it might be necessary.

Did he imagine she'd forgotten? That was an insult in itself.

It had only been three years and he'd changed little. His hair was still dark, the face angular, blue eyes as mocking as ever. The most beautiful man in the universe—that was what her sister Pen called him—and she wasn't far off. It was just a pity that he was a complete bastard.

'Yes?' She matched his haughty tone, although hers wasn't innate. She hadn't been born sucking on a silver spoon.

He stooped to pick up the key she'd dropped. 'May I come in?'

'Do I have a choice?' she muttered at the action.

'Of course.' He handed her back the Yale, then stated shortly, 'It's about Pen.'

She had assumed as much. His brother Tom was married to her sister Pen. She wondered if Pen had done something silly again.

His expression was closed, giving nothing away. 'Look, can we do this inside?'

'Can't it keep?' she appealed. 'I'm tired.'

He noted the shadows under her eyes, even as he replied, 'No, it can't.'

'Oh, all right.' Reluctantly she unlocked the door and let him follow her into the hall. 'But if we can make this brief, because I really am exhausted.'

His mouth twisted. 'Busy weekend?'

'Somewhat.' She wasn't about to go into it; let him think what she liked. He usually did.

'I've been phoning you since first thing yesterday,' he informed her in repressive tones.

'I was out.'

'So I gathered.'

On the town, that was what he imagined. That she had some high social life, the last of the good-time girls. She should be so lucky.

'*At work,*' she stressed.

'At six in the morning?' He clearly didn't believe her.

It was true, however. Cass had been on call and slept Friday and Saturday in a room in the hospital.

She gave up defending herself and said, 'Is this really any of your business?'

Dark brows gathered in displeasure and his mouth thinned, but he surprised her by backing down.

'No, possibly not,' he agreed, before adding, 'If we could go and sit somewhere...?'

He took off his coat, waiting for her to hang it up.

Her reluctance couldn't have been plainer as she stood, dripping in her own wet clothes and guarding the living-room door.

'I'm not going to leap on you, you know,' he stated with an impatient edge.

The thought hadn't entered her mind, but now it did, it hung between them. Not that he'd *ever* leapt on her. It had been more a mutual thing.

Their eyes met for a second, acknowledging, remembering, then burying the emotions that had briefly coloured their relationship.

She finally took his coat from him and put it on a hook on the wall, then led the way through to the living room.

It always looked shabby, with its odds and ends of furniture bought at junk shops, inherited from friends or simply rescued from skips. He made it look shabbier, dressed as he was in silk shirt and tailored grey suit of impeccable cut.

He was overdressed for a casual visit to her, and the niggle of a bad feeling in her stomach became worse. Was Pen in some kind of trouble?

She watched as he adjusted his long, supple frame in one of her old armchairs and waited for him to speak.

He ran a critical eye over her, too, saying, 'If you want to change and get dry first, I'll wait.'

'No, I'm fine.' She took off her jacket and threw it over the back of a chair. The blue cotton shirt underneath was damp, as were her navy trousers, but she decided to live with the discomfort. 'Do you want a drink?' she asked out of mere politeness.

It was a surprise when he accepted. 'A small whisky if you have it.'

She'd meant tea, but she crouched down to what passed for a drinks-cabinet in the bottom of the sideboard. 'I'm afraid it's vodka and lemonade or martini.'

'Vodka—as it comes.' He said it like a man who needed a drink, and, when she took out only one glass, added, 'I think you should pour yourself one, too.'

Definitely bad news, but then what other kind would this man bring her?

She did what he said, sloshing a little lemonade in her vodka to make it drinkable, and placed his glass on the coffee-table in front of him, before taking the chair opposite.

She watched him fortify himself with a mouthful of liquor, then look across at her, searching for the right words to use, and she realised this wasn't about some stupid thing Pen had done.

Her sense of *déjà vu* was too strong. Just that afternoon she'd had to tell a sobbing mother her son was dead, hoping the woman would guess before she had to say the words aloud.

'Something's happened to Pen, hasn't it?' she said to Drayton Carlisle now.

He nodded his head. 'I don't know how to tell you this—'

'She's dead.' Cass said the words quickly, then prayed for an equally quick denial.

He looked surprised and gave her brief hope that she was being overly dramatic. Then he took it away as he nodded once more.

He began to speak, to go into detail, but the blood was rushing to Cass's head and she couldn't hear what he was saying. She knew she was on the verge of fainting and took a deep breath to steady herself. By sheer force of will, she brought herself back from oblivion, and forced herself to concentrate on his voice.

'The results should be known by Tuesday,' he concluded gravely.

'The results?' Cass had missed most of the rest.

He frowned as he repeated, 'Of the *post mortem*.'

'They can't do that!' Cass was horrified for Pen. Beautiful Pen, so proud of her looks, her model-girl figure.

'They have to,' Drayton Carlisle told her quietly, 'in cases of unexpected deaths.'

Cass understood that. She just wasn't thinking on a logical level. The first shock was followed by a sense of unreality.

That sense intensified as he added, 'Tom says you may not have known about the baby.'

'The baby?' she echoed warily—was Pen's secret finally out?

Drayton Carlisle gave her a puzzled look in return. He'd just explained.

'The baby she was carrying,' he reminded her. 'It's a girl. She's in special care.'

Cass shook her head in disbelief—Pen had been pregnant again?

'You didn't know, did you?' he concluded from her expression.

Disbelief gave way to anger as Cass muttered aloud, 'The stupid, stupid girl!'

Drayton Carlisle's mouth curved with renewed contempt. 'Presumably she anticipated your reaction.'

'I'm sure she did.' Cass recalled the last conversation she'd had with Pen on the subject. She had warned her then, but of course Pen had never listened.

'She told Tom you might have a problem with it,' Drayton Carlisle ran on.

That was an understatement. She caught Drayton Carlisle watching her, drawing quite the wrong conclusions. The truth would have vindicated her but how could she reveal it when Pen had paid the ultimate price for her lies?

'What's the prognosis?' she asked instead.

'Prognosis?'

'For the baby.'

He frowned at the clinical term, before relaying, 'She's a good size for a premature baby so they're cautiously optimistic.'

Cass nodded but wouldn't ask more.

'How is Tom?' she added instead.

Mention of his brother made Drayton Carlisle's face grow grimmer.

'Coping,' he claimed briefly.

Cass doubted it. She thought of Tom Carlisle—less arrogant than big brother, slightly immature, more likeable for his insecurities.

'I've arranged the funeral for Wednesday,' Drayton Carlisle informed her, an indication, perhaps, of the true state of affairs. *He* had arranged, not Tom.

'Cremation.' Cass checked he had it right.

He raised a brow at her insistent tone. 'No, burial… Why?'

'That's not what she'd want.'

'How do you know?'

It could have been a genuine question but Cass didn't think so. He meant: how did she know when she'd had minimal contact with her sister over the last few years?

But she did. She knew her sister better than any of them.

She had lived with the real girl, not the sanitised version that had been desperate to become a member of the Carlisle clan.

'You can't bury her,' Cass repeated. 'She had this thing about it, after our mother died. About bodies rotting in the ground.'

He still looked doubtful. 'I'll check with Tom.'

'Do that if you want—' she scowled back '—but I'm telling you. She'd want to be cremated.'

'If Tom agrees,' he conceded, then went on to relay, 'It'll just be a small private funeral, family only.'

She shook her head again. 'That's not what Pen would have liked, either.'

This time his face reflected annoyance as he ceased making concessions for her possible grief. Her hard-bitten tones suggested she felt none, anyway.

'Forgive me, but can you really be the judge of that?' he countered. 'It's not as if you and Pen were very close.'

Statement or accusation? Cass returned his hard glance. She owed him no explanation of her somewhat complex relationship with Pen.

'Possibly not,' she conceded. 'I just happen to know her attitude towards funerals. At our mother's, she found it pitiful that there were only a handful of mourners and swore she'd have hundreds at her own. She was only fifteen at the time—' Cass paused and swallowed hard, determined to hold it together in front of this man '—but I imagine those sentiments stand. Unless Pen suddenly became the shy retiring type?'

'Hardly.' Drayton Carlisle's mouth thinned at the idea. 'I was thinking of Tom when I arranged the funeral.'

'And I'm thinking of my sister,' Cass replied.

They abandoned their uneasy truce and exchanged hostile stares.

'And I'm paying for it,' he pointed out.

End of argument.

Cass's lip curled. 'You're such a louse, Carlisle.'

He grimaced briefly, before countering, 'And you're the hardest woman I have ever met in my life.'

Deep down it hurt. No woman liked to be called hard. Cass, however, was a past master at hiding her feelings.

'How kind of you to say so,' she retaliated.

'That wasn't meant as a compliment.'

'I know.'

They traded stares again. Anger was prevalent for a moment, but it gave way to intrigue as each wondered what made the other tick.

Cass was the first to look away. 'I'll see you out.'

She rose abruptly and he followed. In the hall, they turned at virtually the same moment to reach for his coat and collided a little. The first to recover, Drayton Carlisle put a steadying hand on Cass's arm.

That was all. But his touch still burned and she recoiled from it as if it were an assault.

'I wasn't going to hurt you,' he ground out in a voice tight with control.

'As if,' Cass threw back, angry at her own lack of self-possession.

Perhaps Pen had been right. She was turning into an uptight spinster.

'No, of course.' Drayton Carlisle's thoughts were on Pen, too, as he relayed, 'Your sister always said you were scared of nothing and cared about even less.'

Cass could just hear her sister say the words. She shut her eyes but could still hear them. Tough talk, but quite untrue. Surely Pen had known that she'd cared desperately about *her*?

Drayton Carlisle watched, at first a detached observer. Finally it was there. Pain etched on her beautiful, high-boned face. He'd wanted it there, to see if the girl he'd briefly known—the girl who could feel and laugh and love—had been real, yet he relented almost immediately as she lifted an anguished hand to her mouth.

'I'm sorry. I shouldn't have said that—' he reached an arm out '—it's not even tr—'

'It doesn't matter!' Cass shook her head before he could retract it. Pointless, anyway. What he'd said was undeniably Pen, a throwaway remark that hurt less than the echoes of her sister's voice, suddenly destroying her composure.

Tears gathered at the back of her eyes, tore at her throat, threatened to spill too soon, as it finally got through to her, past barriers of self-preservation and years of professional training. Pen was dead. Not just missing for a while. She was never going to sail back into her life, maddening one moment, charming the next, reckless and lovable and, to Cass's eyes only, so very vulnerable.

'I have to—' Cass couldn't get the words out but she made to retreat.

He caught hold of her arm again. 'Listen to me, Cass. I was lying,' he insisted, 'and you're right—I am a louse.'

Just not a total one, Cass realised, unnerved by his turn-around.

'It d-doesn't m-matter.' She couldn't explain. 'N-none of it matters. I—I...' She shut tight her eyes but the tears leaked from them, anyway.

A low, 'Damn,' came from Drayton Carlisle, but, if it was exasperation, he wouldn't let her turn away.

She tried, only he held her too tightly. She pushed at his shoulders, then actually struck him, when she could no longer stifle her sobs. He let her, offering her something, *somebody* to rage against in her grief, but she didn't seem to have the strength. She struck him once more before she suddenly turned into a sobbing pathetic mess in his arms.

She cried for what seemed like an age, her head buried in his shoulder, her hands twisted into the folds of his jacket, and he held her in his arms; for a while their closeness was as natural as breathing. But when there were no more tears left to cry and she sobered up, it was as awkward as a first clinch with a boy.

More so, perhaps, because this wasn't her first clinch with him.

'I'm okay now.' She lifted her head away.

'Good.' He was looking down at her, but she refused to look up.

She spoke to his shoulder. 'Please go. I have some calls to make, people to tell.'

'I could do it,' he offered surprisingly.

'No! No, thank you,' she tempered her rejection.

'All right.' He didn't insist but gently pressed her arm as he said, 'Look, I really am sorry—'

'It's okay, honestly,' she stopped him before he could go on. 'Pen says—*said* worse to my face. It just sounded so like her, that was all… About the funeral—'

'If Tom agrees, we'll make it public.'

'You're right, of course. It's up to him. But what I was about to say is: I can't go.'

'What?' He was clearly shocked.

'I can't go,' she repeated as the hand on her arm finally dropped away.

She couldn't stand at a graveside and bury her sister. It was too hard. No matter that things hadn't always been right between them.

'I'm on duty all week,' she claimed as an excuse.

Drayton Carlisle stared at her as if she were mad. 'The supermarket could surely spare you for a day.'

Cass stared back, questioning his sanity in turn. Then she realised. Pen hadn't told them of her career change. Why was that?

'All right, I *won't* go,' she said with blunt honesty. 'Satisfied?'

Drayton Carlisle shook his head. It was hard to reconcile

this Cass Barker with the one who had been crying in his arms just a few minutes ago.

'I don't understand you, but then I never did.'

'Did you try?'

It slipped out before Cass could stop it. She heard her own bitterness and was scared of giving more away.

She turned from him and opened the door. She held it wide, waiting for him to leave.

He took the hint, putting on his coat and walking towards the door, but said as he drew level, 'We haven't resolved this yet. I'll call tomorrow.'

Cass shrugged, as if to say, Do what you like. Tomorrow she might be up to the fight. Tonight she just wanted him to go before she broke down again.

His eyes rested on her a moment longer, intense, searing blue eyes, then he was gone. Thank God.

She closed the door and leaned heavily against it, drained of strength and anger.

Another death to face. It felt like familiar territory. Perhaps because it was. Father. Mother. Sister. Hard not to take personally. Why me? Why us? Why Pen?

She went back through to the sideboard and took out the family photograph album. It contained a record of their lives before their father's death from cancer when Cass was fifteen and Pen nine. Here were the memories of happy holidays and birthday parties and dressing up for school plays.

These photographs had always made Cass a little mournful. Now, as she turned page after page, and saw Pen, a blonde-haired angel, smiling into cameras, sitting on knees, pulling faces, she felt utterly bereft. This time, when she cried, her grief was for all of them, for her beloved little sister and her strong, clever father and her pretty, laughing mother, and even for herself, the once carefree child she'd been.

The guilt came stealing in later, and, with it, that familiar question: what should I have done? It seemed she'd been asking it for ever. It seemed she'd always got it wrong.

She'd gone away to study medicine at university, imagining that one day she would provide her widowed mother with a better life. When her mother had died in a road accident, how she'd wished she'd never gone away!

The only thing that had kept her from folding then had been her sister. In those first hours and days she had held Pen and comforted her and they had been so close it was hard to imagine they would ever be anything else.

Reality, however, had come to call on the afternoon they had buried their mother. It had been in the shape of a boy, more Cass's age than Pen's. Cass had taken in the earring and tattoo and the sullen manner, and stood, aghast, while Pen had grabbed a coat and disappeared before she'd been able to do anything. It had seemed that, in Cass's absence, Pen had grown up fast—too fast.

When Pen had finally reappeared at two in the morning, Cass's mind had been made up. She wouldn't abandon Pen to a life of no-hope boyfriends and, for want of any willing relatives, a year in care. Surely she could do better?

She had fully believed so and had transplanted what had been left of the family to this tiny terraced house in London. Pen had protested loudly and had managed to sulk continuously for a fortnight in between tearful phone calls to the boyfriend. Then gradually she had made friends at her new school and had stopped pining for Pontefract, and Cass had breathed a sigh of relief.

That relief had been short-lived. Within a couple of months, Pen had been going up West—to nightclubs and bars where looks had counted more than birth dates—and Cass had been left to wonder how she could possibly control her.

All those years gone by and Cass still didn't know the right answer. She just felt if she'd done it, Pen might still be alive.

CHAPTER TWO

WORK was Cass's salvation. Having finally fallen asleep in the small hours, she was woken at seven a.m. by her pager bleeping. It was the hospital. One of the A and E doctors was himself sick. Would Cass cover for him? She agreed readily. Anything rather than spend a day brooding on her sister's death.

She told no one and no one would have guessed the serious-faced Dr Barker had cried herself to sleep. She stitched cuts, pumped stomachs, jump-started a heart, all with her normal cool efficiency.

Of course, grief didn't go away. She put it on hold while she worked the accident unit and coped with other people's pain, but it returned the moment she was home.

She managed to make phone calls to a great aunt and her mother's cousin—the only known relatives left—before the cousin's well-meaning words overwhelmed her. When the phone rang shortly afterwards, she didn't pick it up. She was crying too hard to talk to anyone.

It was much later when she remembered the call and lifted the receiver to find a message had been left for her. In fact, there were three messages, timed throughout the day, each more terse than the last. They were all from Drayton Carlisle, requesting that she call him on his mobile to discuss funeral arrangements.

He had obviously lost what little sympathy he'd had for her. Cass told herself she didn't care. She didn't need his concern. He had never understood her or her relationship with Pen. He knew nothing of the past which had linked them inextricably before driving them apart.

Sometimes secrets did that to families. Pen had wanted to take hers and parcel it up tight and bury it so deep no one would ever discover it. The trouble was Cass. Cass knew the secret, had lived with it, helped her over it. Cass would have kept it, too, but Pen had never been sure of that. Pen hadn't been able to keep other people's secrets. She'd assumed Cass was the same and lived in fear of the day Cass would tell. So Pen had kept her at a distance, away from the Carlisle family and her new life.

Cass had accepted this, because she felt partly responsible for the past. If she'd controlled Pen better, she wouldn't have been pregnant at sixteen, five months gone before realising, sobbing her heart out and suddenly a little girl again. Cass had concealed her own horror and offered comfort rather than recrimination until Pen had become resigned, then excited about the life moving inside her. She'd talked endlessly of possible names and impossibly expensive baby clothes.

It was not to be, however. The baby had made a sudden entrance to the world in a bedroom upstairs. He had struggled and gasped for life. Cass had tried and failed to breathe life into his small perfect body. Pen had been left empty-armed and devastated.

Cass, questioning her very vocation, had abandoned her studies to concentrate on getting Pen through the dark times. For a while it had seemed her sister would stay broken, defeated, unable to get over the pain of it, but in time she had emerged from the whole affair with a new, tougher edge.

Pen had decided she wanted to be a model. Cass had quelled any doubts and happily paid for a portfolio of photographs—anything rather than have Pen aimlessly sitting around. She'd sold her textbooks and stethoscope, believing she'd never go back to medicine. It had been money well spent when Pen had come home in seventh heaven at having been accepted on the books of a modelling agency.

But dreams of being a supermodel hadn't quite become

reality. Pen hadn't been tall enough for catwalk and had been too slim for glamour. She'd managed to win a few catalogue assignments, mostly for the teen market, and when they'd dried up she'd settled for PR work at trade shows.

It had been through promotional work she'd met the Carlisles and, almost from day one, what had once been a joke—marrying money—had turned into a mission statement. Initially the talk had been of a Drayton Carlisle until Pen had decided he was too ancient and had subsequently transferred her affections to his younger brother, Tom.

Cass should have been appalled and had been really, but it had kept Pen happy. She hadn't anticipated Pen being successful. Pen had still been only seventeen and, though scarred by experience, had been surely transparent to any man with insight.

She hadn't reckoned on Thomson Carlisle. Some years older than Pen, but oddly immature. A privileged childhood fractured by the loss of his parents. Sweet, if a little weak-natured.

Had Pen loved Tom Carlisle? Cass had never been certain. Pen had appeared in triumph, waving a diamond engagement ring. At that point Tom had been an unknown quantity, and Pen had been infuriatingly vague. He'd been around twenty-two or -three or -four, had had a flat somewhere in South Ken and had been something in the family engineering business. She'd been more specific about the sporty Merc he'd driven and his two hundred and fifty thousand pounds a year trust fund.

In fact, Cass hadn't met Tom first, but Drayton Carlisle. He had appeared on the doorstep one evening, this tall, immaculately dressed, studiously polite, breathtakingly handsome creature from another planet. Cass had felt this curious twisting sensation in her stomach, seconds before her normal barriers had gone up.

She'd already been in a bad mood; his uninvited presence

had put her in worse. She'd spent the day cleaning the house and worrying about Pen who had been out all night, and in ten minutes she'd been due to start an evening shift as a checkout girl at the local supermarket where she'd been working since abandoning her studies.

'Yes?' she'd fairly barked the word at this stranger.

He returned politely. 'I'm not sure if I have the right address. I'm looking for a family called Barker.'

'Yes,' Cass repeated, without committing herself.

'Are you Penelope's sister?' he added after studying her face.

He sounded mildly surprised. He'd possibly expected a petite, short-skirted blonde like Pen, and ended up with a tall, nylon-overalled mouse.

'You're Tom?' Cass was surprised, too. This man looked far too mature for Pen.

He shook his head. 'I'd better introduce myself. I'm Drayton Carlisle, Tom's brother. And you are…'

Confused, that was what she was. She had yet to meet Tom and here was his big brother on the doorstep. She smelled a rat.

'Cass,' she replied abruptly.

'Cass?' He checked he had it right, 'That'll be short for…?'

Cass thought it fairly obvious and said with irony, 'Castleford.'

'Castleford?' he repeated quizzically.

'Town up t'North,' she relayed, exaggerating her Yorkshire vowels.

His eyes narrowed briefly. Did he realise she was winding him up?

'How unusual,' he commented dryly.

'And *Drayton* isn't?' she couldn't resist countering.

'Family name,' he grimaced. 'My mother was a Drayton.'

'*Really.*' Cass pretended to be impressed. 'One of *the* Draytons?'

Of course, she'd gone too far. She'd put him down as an upper-class twit. She was right on one count but not the other.

He stared straight at her for a moment. It was an intense scrutiny. His eyes were ice-blue and hard and intelligent.

'More Northern humour, I presume,' he finally concluded before directing at her, 'Is Penelope in?'

'No, sorry.' She shrugged into the jacket already in her hand. 'Is there a message I can pass on?'

'Are you expecting her back soon?' he persisted.

How to answer that? Pen came and Pen went. Cass had long since lost any control over her movements.

Cass confined herself to a shrug.

'In that case, perhaps you and I could have a talk about matters?' he suggested, a hint of steel now behind the polite, well-modulated tones.

Matters being his brother marrying a nobody that he'd known five minutes. Even Cass could see the family would be less than thrilled.

'Look—' she glanced at her watch '—I don't mean to be rude, Mr Carlisle, but can we make it some other time? I have to be in work in fifteen minutes.'

'Is your work close?' he asked as she shut and locked the door behind her.

'A mile or so.' She was going to have to run.

He must have read her mind as he said, 'I'll give you a lift.'

Cass was briefly tempted, before replying, 'It's all right. I can be a little late and I don't want to put you to any bother—'

'It's no bother.' He followed her out on the pavement, and directed a remote unlocking device to the row of cars ahead.

She saw a set of tail-lights briefly illuminate but it wasn't until they were level that she read the logo and had a good look at the sleek sports car.

She kept her face impassive. Pen might be impressed by fast cars but she refused to be.

He opened the passenger door for her, and waited as she debated whether to accept this lift or not. He looked safe. Well, safe as in unlikely to turn out to be a psychopath or safe as even less likely to be interested in girls dressed in supermarket overalls.

She climbed in and found herself sinking into opulent leather. How the other half lived.

She gave him directions and, though it wasn't far, they were caught in the rush hour.

'I wondered—how do you feel about their relationship?' he asked as they inched along the High Street.

'I really can't say.' Cass knew Pen would never forgive her if she did. 'I haven't met your brother.'

'Then you must have some doubts,' he was quick to conclude. 'Your sister's only...what, seventeen? Rather young to be rushing into marriage, don't you think?'

Quite, Cass could have agreed, but she wasn't willing to give him the satisfaction—especially when she remembered Tom wasn't the only Carlisle Pen had gone out with.

'Not too young to be dated by men in their thirties, though,' she said pointedly.

His eyes narrowed briefly from the road to her. 'You mean me?'

'Who else?'

'That was once only.'

'Well, that's all right, then,' Cass returned with heavy irony.

'No, it isn't—' he sounded annoyed '—and I didn't *date* her. The company had an exhibition stand at Earls Court. I took those involved to dinner on the final day and somehow ended up with your sister. When I discovered how young she was—not to mention immature—I sent her home in a taxi, *unsullied*.'

Cass swivelled her head in his direction and saw from his tight-lipped expression he was being totally serious.

She felt an odd rush of relief, although she was not quite sure why. If Pen hadn't slept with this man, there were others.

'I'll take your word for it,' she finally said.

'*Do*,' he said with insistence, before shifting back to his original argument. 'At any rate, I'd say she's too young for commitment.'

'Really,' she replied archly. 'How kind of you to be concerned for her.'

His eyes went from the road to Cass, checking if she were that naive. The curve of her lips told him otherwise.

'Yes, all right, it's obviously my brother's interests I'm protecting,' he admitted.

'Or even his trust fund,' she suggested somewhat recklessly.

He was quick to observe, 'You know about his fund, do you?'

Cass could have kicked herself. She'd never met his brother yet she knew his financial situation!

She shrugged as if it had been just a guess. 'All you rich types have trust funds, don't you? Turn left here, by the way,' she added, relieved to see they'd arrived.

He drove into the supermarket car park and Cass jumped out the moment he drew into a bay, muttering an offhand, 'Thanks,' as she went.

He wasn't so easily dismissed, however. A detaining hand was laid on her arm before she reached the outer door.

'I'm late,' she protested.

'Tough.' Unmoved, he resumed their conversation. 'So, having a trust fund, that makes Tom fair game, does it?'

'I didn't say that.' Cass tried and failed to shrug off his hand.

He tightened his grip. 'But you think it.'

Cass's temper rose along with his. 'Pardon me, but have we *met* before?'

He frowned at this *non sequitur*. 'Not that I can remember.'

'No,' she said archly, 'so what makes you an expert on how I think?'

It stopped him in his tracks for a moment and a cloud gathered over his high, handsome brow. Cass waited for it to descend on her but, though their eyes met and clashed, he surprised her with his reaction.

'You're right. I was being presumptuous,' he finally responded. 'Perhaps you could clue me into how you really feel?'

Cass didn't see that she could, *and* be loyal to her sister, so she dodged the question and said instead, 'I don't know how old your brother is—'

'Twenty-five—' was supplied.

'But I imagine, like my sister, he'll do what he wants, regardless,' she ran on.

'Not necessarily,' he countered. 'Not if he considers who controls his trust fund.'

His tone was understated, but his meaning was obvious.

'You,' she concluded.

'Me.' He nodded.

The fact wasn't of much importance to Cass but she wondered if her sister knew it.

'Possibly Tom has been reticent on the subject,' Drayton Carlisle continued smoothly, 'but I feel one should be straight about these things.'

He smiled as if they might have reached some understanding but the smile never reached those chilly blue eyes.

Cass checked she really had understood. 'Let's see if I

have this right. You want me to toddle off home tonight and tell Pen who's holding the purse-strings, while you sit back and hope she transfers her affections elsewhere. Is that straight enough for you?'

She raised challenging green eyes to his, but this time he surprised her with a dry laugh.

'Frighteningly accurate,' he conceded with the slight inclination of his head, before drawling on, 'I wonder if the expression *too clever for your own good* has ever been run past you.'

'Once or twice,' she admitted, 'but I don't let it bother me...insecure men have never been my thing.'

He laughed again, any insult bouncing off him. It was hardly surprising. This handsome, he'd probably never had a moment's self-doubt.

She was aware of his eyes doing a quick inventory, looking beyond her scraped-back hair and the shapeless nylon uniform she wore.

'So, what kind are?' he asked, and this time his interest was personal.

'Why?' Cass didn't want to play these games.

'No reason.' He shrugged. 'I just wondered if there's a man in your life.'

'Several,' she claimed rather than tell the sad truth. 'They're queuing up, in fact.'

He followed her glance towards the crowded checkout tills inside and laughed in reply. 'I'd better let you go, then. When are you finished?'

'Eight... Why?'

'I thought I'd take you for a drink.'

He smiled. It was slow and amused. Cass wondered how many women had fallen for just that smile.

For a mad moment she was tempted. Perhaps it would be fun, cutting him down to size.

Then she remembered. 'I can't.'

'Or won't?' he drawled back.

It really was 'can't'. After the supermarket Cass went on to a night shift at the Happy Hamburger.

But Cass was unwilling to explain herself and shrugged instead. 'Whichever.'

He seemed unmoved, muttering, 'Another time.'

Just words, Cass assumed, until their eyes met, trading silent messages, and she realised he meant it. There *would* be another time. He would make sure of that.

For a moment the promise—or threat—held her there, fascinated when she should have been repelled, then he was gone and only the scent of male power remained.

Too late for a clever put-down, even if she could have thought of one. She consoled herself with the thought that their paths were unlikely to cross again.

Of course she relayed their conversation to Pen, only Pen didn't listen. Or didn't appear to. Instead she looked like the cat that'd licked the cream and boasted that she could handle Dray. Although Cass repeated content and underlying meaning, Pen's confidence remained. In fact, with breathtaking ego, she suggested that Drayton Carlisle's objections were rooted in jealousy because he'd dated her first and was still interested.

Pen clearly believed this, and, worse, seemed excited by the prospect. Cass tried to talk sense to her, to say without actually saying it that a man like Drayton Carlisle—smart, mature, attractive—might want slightly more from a female companion than teenage youth. Pen, in turn, accused *her* of jealousy, too, of being piqued because he would never look at her.

Normally Cass quit arguments with Pen when they descended onto such a petty level but this time she fought back and admitted that Drayton Carlisle had done more than look—he'd asked her out.

It stopped Pen in her tracks and she just stared at Cass for a long moment, as if she were a stranger, before giving a caustic laugh and claiming Drayton Carlisle had been amusing himself.

Cass, who'd already worked out that possibility, didn't feel like thanking Pen for underlining it, and, for once, was the one to walk out in temper.

Pen realised she'd gone too far and later issued quite a sweet apology. She hadn't meant the comment personally. It was just that Drayton Carlisle had a bad reputation where women were concerned and she'd hate for Cass to be one of his victims. She sounded so sincere that Cass accepted this explanation and they made up.

They'd never really fallen out again but she'd still pretty much lost her sister from the day three years ago when she'd married Tom Carlisle. Sometimes they'd met up in London after Pen had spent the day shopping (it seemed that Tom's allowance had not been stopped) and Cass had tried to make the right noises when Pen had shown her the latest bag or must-have shoes. It had been hard, however, as designer labels had been of minimal interest to Cass while the accompanying price tags could have brought tears to the eyes.

Cass had returned to her studies, by then, and had a mounting overdraft despite moonlighting at a pizza parlour. Of course she could have asked Pen for money. Once or twice Pen had offered. The trouble was Cass had never seen it as Pen's money. It would always be Carlisle money and the idea of Drayton Carlisle discovering she'd accepted a handout had kept her from doing so. Not that Pen had ever mentioned her brother-in-law. She'd known it had been a taboo subject with Cass since the time…

Cass didn't complete the thought but was dragged back into the present by the insistent ringing of the telephone. She guessed who it would be before she picked up the receiver but she was ready for him now. There was nothing like a trawl through the past to harden the heart and stiffen the spine.

'It's Drayton,' he announced briefly.

She was even briefer. 'Yes.'

'The funeral has been rearranged for Thursday,' he relayed. 'Tom confirmed your sister's preference for cremation.'

'Right.' Cass remained noncommittal.

'You will go?' he added in equally restrained tones.

If he'd issued a command, she might still have refused, but guilt and duty had been working on her since last night.

'Yes, I'll go,' she agreed simply.

'Good.' He sounded satisfied.

'How's Tom?' she asked, genuinely concerned.

He hesitated, then admitted, 'Distraught.'

It was more honest than he'd been last night. She wanted to ask more, to ask about the baby, but wouldn't let herself.

'In fact, Tom's very anxious to see you,' Dray Carlisle continued in the same vein. 'If you could stay after the funeral, I'd...I'd be grateful.'

Cass frowned down the phone line. Polite on the surface, it was clearly forced. For Tom's sake. But why?

'I'm sorry. I'm on duty in the evening.' It was the truth.

'I see,' he accepted it, as he revealed, 'Tom tells me you now work in a hospital as an orderly.'

An *orderly*? Six years' slog and study dismissed in one word. Thank you, Pen. Why hadn't she told them?

'Something like that,' she replied because it was easier than explanations.

'Which hospital?'

'Why?'

Cass wondered whether he doubted that she worked in a hospital at all.

'I thought I could drive you back down after the funeral,'

he explained, 'if you were prepared to stay and talk with Tom for a while.'

Cass frowned once more. Not at what he was saying, but what he wasn't. If Tom wanted to talk, why hadn't he called himself? And why had Big Brother volunteered, when it was obviously choking him to be conciliatory?

'I don't know.' She had very unsettling memories of North Dean Hall, country seat of the Carlisles. 'I can't be late.'

'On the day of your only sister's funeral,' he clipped back, 'I don't think anybody will be too critical of your timekeeping, do you?'

That was if she told them, which she hadn't and didn't plan to. Bad enough that this man thought she was unnatural. She couldn't and wouldn't expose her grief to the rest of the world.

'Well, that's where you're wrong.' She thought of Hunter-Davies, the consultant for whom she currently slaved. He wouldn't listen to excuses, tolerate mistakes or accept anything less than total commitment. 'My boss wouldn't care where I'd been, and, as I'm coming to the end of my contract, I need a decent reference.'

'*Contract?*' he echoed with renewed suspicion. 'What exactly is it you do?'

It was too direct a question to duck, and, anyway, wasn't there a chance he'd discovered the truth?

'I'm a doctor.' There was an element of pride in her voice.

She expected him to be at least mildly impressed. After all, he'd pretty much written her off as a no-hoper.

But he merely responded, 'Okay, so don't tell me,' assuming she was being sarcastic.

Damn him. Was it so unlikely?

'I'll make sure you're back on time,' he went on. 'In fact, I can send a car to collect you in the morning.'

'There's no need,' she told him coldly. 'I've said I'll come.'

'I wasn't doubting it,' he replied heavily. 'I was trying to be helpful, save you relying on the vagaries of public transport.'

It was possible, Cass supposed, but then she remembered the last time she'd let him *help* her. There was always a motive behind Dray Carlisle's apparent kindness.

'Thanks all the same,' she muttered back, 'but I think I can cope with the train. I do, most days. In fact, it may come as a surprise to you, but a large section of the population rely on public transport.'

'Really!' he feigned surprise, then exclaimed dryly, 'Goodness, how the other half live!'

He wasn't serious, of course. He was just trying to wrong-foot her, borrow her lines before she could use them.

'Well, far be it from me to relieve you of your hair shirt,' he added in his deep drawl. 'Would collecting you from the train be permitted?'

Oddly Cass didn't mind his sarcasm. At least it was honest.

'Strain getting too much for you, Dray?'

'The strain?'

'Of being pleasant to me.'

A moment's disconcerted silence followed, and then he actually laughed. 'As a matter of fact, yes, it was. I see you still prefer plain talking, Cassie.'

Cassie. The name struck chords. Perhaps conjured up by *her* slip, calling him Dray. A reminder that for a brief moment in time they'd been close.

'What's wrong with that?' she threw back.

'Nothing at all,' he conceded, before dropping his voice to a lower, more insidious tone. 'In fact, why don't we go the whole distance, Cassie, and stop pretending we're strangers?'

Just words but they had their effect. Twenty-six years old and blushing like a schoolgirl. God, she was pathetic!

She took a deep, steadying breath and reminded herself he couldn't see her blushes. He could only hear her voice, cold as ice as she responded, 'Who's pretending? You don't imagine my sleeping with you makes you any less a stranger.'

There, she'd said it. It was out in the open. He had no power over her now.

A silence followed, as if she'd shocked him, but he came right back at her with, 'Don't worry, you and your sister shattered any illusions I might have had in that direction.'

The illusions had been hers as Cass remembered. She'd been a fool and Pen had wised her up.

'Still, I suppose I should be flattered you even recall our *tryst*—' he used the word in a purely mocking vein '—considering the many that have undoubtedly followed.'

Many? Cass could have challenged with ample justification. There'd been only one. A student doctor and he'd been another unmitigated disaster. But did she want him knowing just how limited her private life was?

'I keep a record,' she claimed instead. 'You're under D...for Disappointing.'

It was a put-down, so why did he laugh?

'Are you sure it wasn't D for Devastating?' he suggested with his usual drawling arrogance, then cut the ground from beneath her by murmuring, 'That's what I have you under.'

Cass's face flamed once more, as a shutter flickered briefly open on a picture of two bodies intimately entwined, and she wondered why she'd ever started this game of truth.

She stopped it abruptly by saying, 'Well, now we've completed that trip down memory lane, do you think we could get back to the matter in hand? Burying my sister, that is,' she added for both their benefits.

'Of course.' He didn't argue with the change of subjects. Perhaps he regretted the deviation, too. 'Phone me later with the train times and I'll send a car to the station... I'm ordering the wreaths tomorrow. I can arrange one from you, if you wish.'

'No, I'll do that.' She didn't want any favours from him.

'All right… Is there any song you wish to suggest for the service?' he added with surprising generosity.

Cass knew her sister's favourites but none was appropriate for the solemnity of the occasion and she said, 'Not really. None you could play at a funeral.'

'Right, I'll just pick a couple of traditional hymns,' he concluded.

Dirges would have been Pen's comment and Cass was prompted to say, 'Why don't you ask Tom if he can think of anything she'd have liked?'

There was some hesitation before he answered obliquely, 'Tom's attention is focused on the baby at the moment.'

The baby. Her niece. Cass could have asked how she was. It would have been the natural thing to do. But any details and the baby would begin to be real for her.

He was clearly waiting for her to ask. When she didn't, he volunteered. 'She's out of the incubator and doing well.'

'Good.' Cass sounded detached, and was determined to remain so.

He asked outright, 'Would you wish to visit her while you're up?'

'There won't be time,' she replied, avoiding point-blank refusal.

But he heard it in her tone, anyway, and remarked, 'I'd forgotten. Pen said babies weren't your thing.'

Cass frowned. Why had Pen said that? It wasn't true at all.

'I don't imagine they're yours, either,' she countered rather than deny it, then, feeling the conversation was becoming too personal once more, switched to saying, 'That's my pager just gone. I have to use the telephone, so if there's nothing else…'

'*Your pager?*' He was obviously wondering why she needed such a thing.

Cass, having found the article still clipped onto the waistband of her trousers, put it on to test, then held it against the receiver so he could have a quick blast in his eardrum.

'*My pager,*' she repeated heavily, before muttering a terse, 'Bye.'

She put the telephone back on its hook, then took it off again just in case he redialled. If he did, he'd get the busy signal, supporting her story.

Not her story, her *lie*, she corrected herself. Just one more to add to the series she'd told the Carlisles, if only tacitly. How she wished now she'd pressed Pen to be honest with Tom, to admit that she'd had that first baby. If she had, perhaps her sister might yet be alive.

But Pen had convinced Cass that, if she let her secret slip, there would be no marriage and, though, at a month short of eighteen, her sister had been ridiculously young to wed, it had seemed a better option than her vamping around on the nightclub scene. When Pen had finally brought Thomson Carlisle home to meet her, Cass had played her part beautifully, being warm and welcoming to a young man who had seemed naive compared to his brother, and doing her best to pretend along with Pen that she'd been the sweet innocent she'd appeared. It hadn't been so hard because Cass had believed Pen had been at heart.

There had still been an eleventh-hour crisis. Her last night of freedom, Pen had spent with Cass in an exclusive hotel, courtesy of the Carlisles. At first Pen had been in high spirits but by bedtime she'd been tearful. She hadn't been sure she'd loved Tom Carlisle the way she should have done. He'd been very good to her and kind and had bought her anything she'd wanted, but had that been enough?

Cass's heart had plummeted. She'd almost come round to being pleased at the idea of the marriage and now this bombshell.

'No, it's not enough,' she had to agree with Pen.

But it wasn't what Pen wanted to hear, as she wailed back,

'What would you know? You've never been in my position. No one's ever wanted to marry you!'

Typical of Pen in crisis; Cass was too used to such remarks to let them hurt.

'I'm not going to argue with you, Pen,' she responded softly. 'You're right. I'm probably sitting on the shelf already, but I'd sooner be on my own than live, day in, day out, with a man I didn't love or respect.'

'Who says I don't love him?' Pen protested mournfully. 'Just what I expected—you're trying to talk me out of it!'

'No, I'm not.' Cass gazed steadily at her sister. 'I want what's best for you, that's all. It's what I've always wanted.'

Cass's tone was so gentle Pen looked briefly ashamed. 'I know that really. I suppose I'm being a cow.'

Cass pulled a face. 'A little bit of one—a calf, maybe.'

It wasn't much of a joke but they both laughed and it eased the tension slightly.

Then Pen said simply, 'Tell me what to do, sis.'

But Cass had no magic answers. 'I can't, Pen. I wish I could. Only you know how you feel about Tom—'

'I *do* love him,' Pen insisted, 'but, well...next to Dray, he seems such a lightweight.'

'Oh, Pen,' Cass groaned aloud. 'You don't really have your eye on his big brother, do you?'

'Of course not.' The denial was slow in coming and didn't quite ring true, especially when Pen ran on, 'But he did fancy me at first. I know he did. If only I hadn't told him I was sixteen—'

'Hold on,' Cass cut in, calculating as she did so, 'you must have been seventeen and a half by then.'

Pen nodded. 'But I thought the younger, the better. Most older guys get off on that.'

Cass made no comment, but shuddered inwardly. What kind of men *had* Pen been dating?

'Not him,' Pen continued, rolling her eyes, 'You know

what he said? ''Come back when you're twenty-one!'' Then he kissed me on the forehead as if I were a three-year-old and sent me home in a taxi.'

'Awful man,' Cass mused, straight-faced, while secretly applauding this show of decency.

'Bloody bossy, as well—' Pen pouted in agreement '—and boring about work. He wouldn't let Tom take more than three weeks for his honeymoon.'

'Really.' Cass managed to sound sympathetic. Three weeks seemed more than generous but letting Pen run down Dray Carlisle had to be a good idea.

It was something of a setback when Pen added, 'The trouble is he's so sexy, too.'

Cass wasn't about to argue. Dray Carlisle definitely fell into the sexy category. But should *Pen* be conscious of this fact when she was about to marry his younger brother the following afternoon? Cass thought not.

Pen caught her sister's expression and quickly backtracked. 'Don't worry. I find lots of men sexy. It doesn't mean I'd do anything about it.'

'Lots of men aren't going to be your next door neighbours,' Cass felt she should point out. 'Dray Carlisle is.'

'So? It's not me who'll be sorry,' Pen claimed, 'but Dray, when he realises what he's missing. I can just see him, growing old and wrinkly, carrying a torch for me until the day he dies.'

Cass wasn't sure if Pen was entirely joking, but she laughed with her, anyway. It was becoming clear that, for all her doubts, Pen was going to become Mrs Tom Carlisle, regardless.

'Should I take it the wedding's on?' Cass enquired dryly.

'What do you think?' Pen smirked back. 'All that money— I'd be crazy not to go through with it.'

'*Pen!*' reproved Cass, but Pen continued to grin as she slipped into bed and snuggled down.

It was Cass who was left to switch off the light and lie awake, long after Pen's breathing told her she'd fallen asleep. But that was the nature of things. Pen had cleared her conscience by talking to Cass and now it was Cass's job to do the worrying.

Meanwhile Pen slept like a log and woke bright and breezy the next morning, talking nineteen to the dozen about the wedding, her honeymoon and the house they would one day buy. And later she floated up the aisle of the fine old medieval church where the Carlisles worshipped, trailed by a coterie of attendants, all cousins of Tom's apart from Pen's best friend, Kelly.

Pen had asked Cass to be a bridesmaid, too, but had looked relieved when Cass had demurred, citing lilac as not her colour and flounces even less her style.

Cass was content to sit in one of the front pews, proud of her sister's beauty, doubts quelled by the look of devotion on Tom Carlisle's face when he turned to his future bride.

Even Dray Carlisle seemed to give the marriage his blessing. Dressed in morning coat and tails, he stood at his brother's side, acting as best man, solemn until the ceremony was over, then, with a smile, embracing his brother and Pen in a circle.

Cass had mixed feelings at the gesture. She was pleased that Pen was to be accepted into the Carlisle fold but it surely meant a degree of loss for her. Pen was embarking on a new life and Cass already suspected from hints dropped that she wanted to keep it quite separate from her old one.

Cass understood why and was losing herself in the crowd outside the church when suddenly Dray Carlisle loomed in view, head and shoulders above most people, nodding acknowledgements to friends as he went, before coming to a halt in front of her.

'I've been looking for you everywhere,' he announced without preamble.

Considering they hadn't spoken since the day they'd met, it was hardly the politest of greetings, so why had she felt it again, that sharp pull of attraction?

She hid the fact well, muttering back, 'And it's nice to see you again, too.'

His brow lifted, registering the sarcasm, then he took her arm and instructed briskly, 'Come on.'

'Come on where?' she echoed as he steered her through the crowd.

'Photographs.'

'Oh.'

Cass's lack of enthusiasm was almost tangible.

He squinted her a curious look. 'Don't you want to be included in a record of the happy occasion?'

'Not especially. I'm a little camera shy,' she excused lamely.

'It's only a couple of group photographs,' he assured her as they skirted round the corner of the church to find bride and groom posing against a backdrop of a blossoming cherry tree.

Pen was obviously loving every moment, flirting with the camera in a rather unbridal manner.

'Well, your reticence is clearly not a genetic condition,' Dray Carlisle added in an undertone.

Cass took it as criticism and replied a little sharply, 'Pen's enjoying her day. What's wrong with that?'

'Nothing, I suppose,' he agreed, choosing to be conciliatory. 'I was merely remarking on how different you are.'

'Well, I'm sure if I was drop-dead gorgeous,' Cass stated dryly, 'I'd be tempted to show off a little, too.'

Dray Carlisle might have taken the comment for envy, but he was too astute for that.

'Would you?' He studied her openly for a moment: dark hair, green eyes, classic bone structure and a mouth that was wide and generous even as she tried to turn it into a disapproving line. 'No, I don't think so. Your looks may not be as obvious as your sister's but many men would find you the more attractive. I suspect you know that. You just don't care.'

He was right, in part. Cass had no interest in being rated on her looks. All the same, his analysis put her more on the defensive.

'And you've gathered all this from two minutes' conversation?' she returned in disparaging tones.

'Not quite,' he admitted. 'Pen has talked about you.'

'Oh, right.' Cass could imagine the impression Pen had given of her.

Strait-laced. Inhibited. Repressed, even. Somewhere on that continuum, anyway.

She didn't get a chance to enquire further, as the photographer called out, 'Immediate family, please.'

'Our cue, I believe,' he prompted, when she made no move to step forward.

'Doesn't that mean parents?' She nodded towards the couple already taking up stance beside Tom.

She'd seen them earlier in church, a tall straight-backed gentleman with grey hair and beard and a rather worldlier looking woman dressed in a lemon silk two-piece and an enormous hat.

'That's our Uncle Charles,' he identified the man with a slight smile, before adding with a grimace, 'along with our stepmother, Monica, who is insisting on being in this photograph regardless of the fact she and Tom can barely tolerate each other. So, as you see, neither side can field the conventional line-up, and I'm sure Penelope will want you in it as closest family.'

Cass didn't totally share his confidence but he was already making the decision for her, his hand suddenly clasping hers, pulling her behind him.

The contact was fleeting but her reaction was not. Long after he positioned her by Pen's side and reminded her with gentle irony to smile—it wasn't a funeral—she could feel the warmth and strength of his fingers.

It was then she should have run, of course. Had her photograph taken. Wished her sister well. Called a taxi and caught the first train back to town.

But fool that she was, she had to stay. Had to ignore every dictate of good sense just to find out if it was real, that rush of feeling she'd had when he'd touched her hand.

Real enough, she supposed, only now, three years on, she didn't feel the need to give it a nice name. Maybe it still began with L and had four letters but that was all it had in common with love, that tortured, destructive feeling she'd had for Dray Carlisle.

She thanked God it had ended when it had, in a matter of a few short weeks. Thanked Pen for once having been the wiser sister when her own head had been in a state of mush and her body hurting more than her pride.

It had been like a fever, burning hot and fierce and sending her a little crazy. Then it had suddenly been over. But it had left her weak and fragile for a long time.

She was better now, of course, and immune. Only anger lingered and that was no bad thing. For angry, she was usually cold and detached, and, in that mood, she might just be able to get through another funeral without breaking down.

After it, she would grieve alone for her pretty little sister.

CHAPTER THREE

CASS didn't call North Dean Hall to be picked up at the station. Instead she took a taxi and barely made the crematorium in time.

The Carlisles were *en masse* at the front. Drayton Carlisle saw her enter and indicated she should join them but she slipped into a chair at the back of the chapel. She wasn't family, not really.

The service was a curiously sterile affair. The clergyman spoke of Pen as a devoted wife and homemaker and young mother-to-be, his eulogy full of platitudes and quite erroneous virtues, followed by a dirge of a hymn that Pen would have giggled through if she'd been there beside Cass.

It was thinking of the real Pen that made tears gather at the back of Cass's eyes and she swallowed hard. If she started crying, she wouldn't be able to stop.

There were others sniffing into handkerchiefs, perhaps friends of Pen from the exclusive country club she and Tom had frequented. Cass noticed two heavily pregnant women and wondered if Pen's death had left them anxious.

Cass could have reassured them: few women died in childbirth these days. Just ones with conditions like Pen's which took the medical profession by surprise. And Pen's shouldn't have.

Pen had known the facts. Cass had explained them again last autumn. Pen had lost her first baby due to a womb abnormality and stood a fair chance of losing any others—and her life. Pen had known and chosen to play Russian roulette.

Cass focused on that thought, and kept focusing on it as the priest gave the final blessing and the curtains opened and

40

the coffin slid behind. But it didn't help. She still wanted to shout out at the unfairness of it, cry for the loss of her pretty young sister, scarcely into adulthood.

She wasn't sure if the service was over, but she needed air. She scraped back her chair and made for the door.

She didn't plan it, but, once outside, she had a need to escape altogether. She almost made it—was in sight of the crematorium gates when pursuing footsteps caught up with her.

Drayton Carlisle dispensed with any greeting and went straight to demanding, 'Where the hell do you think you're going?'

Cass would have said it was obvious. 'Back to London.'

'No, you're not!' He grabbed her arm. 'Not yet, anyway. You promised to speak to Tom, remember?'

'I'm not sure what you expect,' she countered. 'I don't know your brother well, and I'm not great at words of comfort.'

He laughed, a brief, harsh sound. 'I can believe that…I don't think it's comfort Tom wants from you. He seems to think you'll know why Pen died.'

Cass frowned. 'Haven't the doctors told him?'

'The medical terms, yes.'

'He wants me to explain those?'

He slid her a look that questioned if she was being deliberately absurd.

'I wouldn't think so,' he returned impatiently. 'Whatever you do at St Wherever, I doubt you're qualified for that.'

'How do you know?' Cass threw back. 'In fact, what do you really know about me? I'll tell you what—'

'Nothing,' he cut in, 'I know nothing about you. I admit it. But this isn't about you and me, it's about Tom. He's holding onto his sanity by a thread, and he seems to believe you're his lifeline. So whatever you think of me, or I think of you, can keep,' he continued, gripping her arm to stop her walking away. 'For now, you come back to North Dean with me and speak to Tom and be damn sure you say the right thing!'

'You can't make me!' Cass protested, even as she found herself being frogmarched back up the drive.

'Can't I?' he muttered through clenched teeth and, as they rejoined the mourners, added in a hiss, 'These people were your sister's friends. At least, behave for her sake.'

Cass felt her face go a dull, angry red. He was treating her like a naughty schoolgirl. He made no allowance for *her* grief, *her* loss.

When he finally released her, she considered another escape bid but then she saw Tom standing with their Uncle Charles and she was too shocked by the sight of him to move. Deep lines were etched on his forehead, ageing him by ten years or more.

He stared at her dully for a moment, then his face contorted on recognition.

'Cass.' He rushed towards her. 'Thank God you came. I need to talk to you. I have to ask you things. You will come back to the house?'

His eyes pleaded with her and there was a desperation in them that had her saying, 'Yes, if you want.'

'Thank you.' He grasped her hands in gratitude. 'And you'll take her away, won't you?'

'Sorry?' Cass made no sense of his question. 'What do you—?'

'Tom, we can't talk about this here,' Dray Carlisle cut in. 'We'll go back to the house…Uncle Charles, will you drive Cassandra?'

'Of course,' his uncle agreed readily.

'You will come?' Drayton directed at her.

She nodded slowly.

His expression remained distrustful, but he didn't press her further. His priority was to get an agitated Tom out of public view.

Cass stared after them, still puzzling over Tom's final words: *You'll take her away*. The her, she assumed, was Pen—or, at least, Pen's ashes. But why? Why would he want her to do that unless he'd discovered the truth? She hoped she was wrong.

Uncle Charles lightly touched her arm and she let him guide her towards an elderly grey saloon car. Eventually they joined the line of cars leaving.

'Good show of people,' Charles remarked.

'Yes.' There had certainly been more mourners than at their mother's funeral.

'Not surprised,' he added gruffly. 'Lovely girl. Always thought so. Poor Tom.'

It came out in short bursts. Their uncle always talked like this. He'd been a naval man and accustomed to issuing information in bulletins.

'He seems very distressed,' Cass concurred.

'Distressed, quite!' Uncle Charles approved the word. 'Still, when he talks to you...' He trailed off on a hopeful note.

Cass said nothing. She couldn't see what she could tell Tom that would make him feel any better.

'How are *you*?' The sympathetic note in his voice recognised her bereaved state.

Cass realised his concern was genuine but her feelings were too complex to express. There was anger in amongst the grief, pity and self-pity, guilt and every other emotion Pen used to draw from her, good and bad. She just needed to bottle it all up so she could get through this bloody awful day.

'Bearing up.' She used a phrase Uncle Charles would understand.

It drew a nod of approval. 'That's all one can do... You will stay overnight?'

Cass feigned polite regret, 'I can't, I'm afraid,' before asking, 'Are you still living in the lodge house?'

'Yes, still there,' he confirmed. 'Don't think I'll be moving now. Ideal for one person. Don't envy Dray, rattling around in that big place on his own.'

'He's not married yet?' Cass had wondered because Pen might not necessarily have told her.

'No, nor likely to be,' was said in fond exasperation. 'Plays the field. Pretty wide one, too, I believe. Not that he tells me much.'

'No one serious, then,' she concluded.

'There was someone a year or so ago,' he relayed. 'Sophie Palmer-Lyons. Grand girl. Good family. Seemed it might come to something.'

Cass told herself she wasn't interested but still asked, 'What happened?'

'Dragged his feet—' his uncle sighed '—so she went off and married someone else... And you? Still seeing the same chap?'

'I—I...no, not now.' Cass was thrown slightly. It was almost two years since her last relationship.

'Oh, well, plenty of time yet,' Uncle Charles reassured her.

To catch a husband, Cass understood he meant, but let it pass. He was from a generation that believed marriage was a woman's goal in life. Forget that his nephew was getting fairly dusty on his own shelf.

Still it was some shelf, Cass reflected as they turned into the gates of North Dean Hall and followed the long drive to the Carlisle country house which was even bigger than she remembered.

There were already several cars parked in the forecourt and people gathered round the doorway where Dray and Tom Carlisle stood.

'Dray's arranged a light buffet for close friends and family,' Uncle Charles relayed as they climbed out of his car.

Cass didn't hide her dismay. Polite conversation and sympathy from people she didn't know. 'I'd rather just have that word with Tom, then go.'

'But surely…well, if that's what you prefer…' He was clearly in a quandary. 'I'll see what Dray says.'

Cass didn't care what Dray said. She didn't want to join the funeral party. She saw a way of avoiding it and took it.

'I'll be down at the summer house,' she said, walking away before anyone could stop her.

She went round the side of the house and through a stone archway to the back terrace. Steps led down to the lawn and she crossed its expanse to a copse of trees and the river beyond.

The summer house had been built as a vantage point to watch the river go by. Of glass and wood, it was showing signs of wear but was still in use, furnished with wicker chairs and tables.

Cass didn't try the door but sat at the top of the steps leading to the jetty by the river.

The sun was hot for the time of year and, discarding the wool jacket of her interview suit, she pushed up the sleeves of the plain blouse beneath. Her feet were hurting, too, in shoes that were rarely worn, but she left them on, feeling some discomfort was appropriate to the day.

Certainly the weather wasn't. She shut her eyes against the glare of the sun and, inevitably, thought of the first time she'd visited North Dean: it had been a similarly glorious day, when her sister had married into the Carlisle family.

Had it been the happiest of Pen's life? Possibly. She'd looked radiant in her white silk wedding gown, and Cass had put aside any lingering worries to feel proud of her lovely sister.

She had not been envious, however. This wasn't the life

for her. She had sat through the wedding meal, bored rigid by a city banker on one side and a Hooray Henry on the other. She would have slipped away after the toast and speeches, but Tom and Dray's Uncle Charles had appeared at her side and insisted on taking her up to the Hall to show her the wedding presents. By the time they had returned, the floor of the marquee had been cleared for dancing.

'You must meet the family.' Uncle Charles guided her over to a table and, seating her, introduced her round to various aunts, cousins and Monica, the stepmother.

The latter declaimed, 'Cassandra? Heavens, what a name!' but the rest were polite enough.

Then the band started to play and all eyes were drawn to the bride and groom as they circled the floor—two beautiful people in love for all the world to see. Cass was possibly alone in hoping the image would turn out to be reality.

The newly-weds were followed onto the floor by Drayton Carlisle and Kelly, the chief bridesmaid. Kelly had already changed out of her demure bridesmaid's gown into a rampantly sexy dress and was, if Cass wasn't mistaken, trying to vamp big brother Carlisle.

Dray didn't exactly look troubled by it. No doubt he was used to women throwing themselves at him.

Cass wasn't aware of staring until Uncle Charles put in, 'Duty dance, my dear. Don't worry.'

'I wasn't…I don't know what you mean,' an unusually flustered Cass responded.

'But I thought…when Dray asked me to…' He trailed off at her continued blank look. 'Sorry. Got it wrong. Forget I spoke. Have a drink.'

He signalled to a passing waiter and pressed a glass of champagne on Cass before embarking on a tale of his naval days.

Cass allowed herself to be distracted and was absorbed in the gruesome wedding customs of a particular South Sea island when Uncle Charles interrupted himself with, 'Ah, here you are!'

It was directed over Cass's head; she didn't have to turn to know Dray Carlisle was there. She wondered how he'd managed to tear himself away from the luscious Kelly.

He went round the table, greeting any relatives he hadn't earlier in the day. A maiden aunt beamed with pleasure when he kissed her cheek and two much younger girl cousins went into gales of laughter at whatever he said to them. He even managed to draw a smile from the stepmother and, on the briefest of acquaintances, Cass realised that was no mean feat. Dray Carlisle was evidently popular with his family as well as with women. It seemed charm *could* get a person everything!

'Have my seat,' Uncle Charles offered, but Dray shook his head, much to Cass's relief.

'Thanks but I feel I should dance with my new sister-in-law first.'

Cass assumed he meant Pen until he came round to her side and curled a hand round her elbow. 'Shall we?'

He didn't wait for a response as he drew her out onto the floor and, encircling her waist, pulled her close enough to dance a slow waltz.

For a beat or two, Cass's heart did somersaults before she effectively stilled it with a vision of Kelly draped similarly in his arms.

'You don't mind?' he asked, rather late. 'I thought you might need rescuing.'

'From your Uncle Charles?' she muttered back. 'Why? Is he a womaniser...*too*?'

His mouth thinned at the question. Any humour in it had passed him by.

'Possibly,' he replied at length. 'Would that make him more or less interesting?'

Now that sounded like a test and Cass couldn't resist answering, 'Depends—is he linked to the Carlisle millions?'

It was sheer cheek. He had to know that.

Yet his murmur of, 'Tenuously,' was followed by a suggestive, 'Perhaps I should have left you in his clutches.'

Cass raised her eyebrows heavenward. Did he really believe she'd be that obvious if she were a gold-digger?

'If you think I'm interested in rich old duffers,' she countered dryly, '*you're* going to be in for a disappointment.'

He saw the insult instantly and it stopped him in his tracks, literally, but then the music had stopped, too.

She made to walk away and he caught her by the arm. 'Is that how you see me?'

Of course it wasn't. He was hardly old for a start—mid-thirties at most. And he was no duffer: this man knew what he wanted from life and made sure he got it. Only the 'rich' bit held, a positive attraction for some women.

Just not Cass.

It really wasn't. Not the money, anyway. The man, well, that was something else.

'I don't know you,' she finally replied.

It was carefully neutral.

The way he looked at her wasn't.

'You will.'

He spoke with utter certainty.

Threat or promise?

A joke, Cass decided. Safer than anything else. She forced a laugh.

'I doubt it. We don't move in the same circles.'

'Is that a problem?'

Not to him, obviously, but then to the rich and powerful, things rarely were.

'It is to me,' she replied with quiet dignity, and waited for him to let her go.

He held her tighter for a moment, fingers warm and hard on her flesh, then he dropped his hand away.

She didn't linger—not when every instinct of self-preservation was telling her to run—but circled back to the table to collect her handbag.

Uncle Charles was still seated there and she murmured a polite, 'It was nice to meet you.'

'You're going? Surely not.' He glanced towards the dance floor.

Cass followed his gaze, not surprised when it homed in on Dray Carlisle. Not surprised, either, to find, with her barely left, another girl had taken her place. No, what surprised her was how bad it made her feel.

Of course, it was even more reason not to get involved. To feel that jealous after one dance and a handful of words. It was frightening.

But it was fascinating, too, and when he stared back at her, across that crowded room, it seemed a very long time before either could look away.

She did it, though. She walked away, too.

If fate hadn't intervened, she would have escaped altogether. But wasn't that the nature of fate—that some things were inescapable?

She was emerging from a rear exit of the marquee when she saw him, a boy waving from the far edge of the lawn. It took her a moment to realise it was at her, and that he wasn't waving but signalling and in some distress as he began running towards her.

She hurried to meet him—faster when she saw his wet clothes—and listened as he sobbed out a story between gasps for breath.

The rest was panic as she raced to the river beyond the lawns and wooded boundary. Shoes flying, dress ripping, half jumping, half falling from the bank. Ignoring the drifting dinghy. Swimming towards flailing arms in the water. Too slow, too late. Diving futilely. Tiring, swallowing, choking.

She was a breath short of drowning herself when strong arms dragged her upwards.

'The boy? He's somewhere round here?' was shouted over the roar in her ears.

She could only nod but it was enough.

'Take her!'

Another set of arms came round her, helping her towards a wooden jetty, leaving the first to search.

Then she was back on dry land, retching and shaking, waiting and praying at each dive made. Seconds, minutes even, ticking by. Hopeless it seemed. Such relief when two heads, not one, suddenly bobbed to the surface.

'Thank God!' came from the man beside her on the jetty and she gave him a surprised look, having almost forgotten he was there. 'I'm Simon, by the way…Simon Carlisle.'

She nodded. They'd met briefly. He was a cousin.

Her eyes returned to Drayton Carlisle as he backstroked the child's limp figure towards them.

They all helped lift the body out of the water. It appeared lifeless but Cass touched her fingers to the neck and found a faint pulse.

'What should one do?' Simon Carlisle asked uncertainly.

Cass was already doing it, expelling water from the boy's lungs before she breathed life back into him. It took time and patience. The men watched in silence until finally the boy spluttered and groaned and regained consciousness.

'Is he fit to carry up to the house?' Drayton Carlisle deferred to her evident knowledge of first aid.

'I—I th-think so.' Her teeth had begun to chatter.

'I'll take him.' Simon Carlisle had already pulled back on the shirt and trousers he'd discarded on the river bank.

Both men had been rational enough to undress before diving into the river. Only Cass had gone in fully clothed and was now paying the penalty as she shivered in her wet cotton dress.

'Here. Take it off and wear this.' Dray handed her his dry white shirt while Simon set off with the boy in his arms.

Cass's hesitation was brief. It wasn't the time for modesty. She turned and he unzipped her dress. It was clammy, ripped and mud-splattered; she dragged it and her tights off. Both were in ruins and she left them on the ground as she slipped on his shirt over her damp skin and underwear, buttoning it as she walked, barefoot, alongside him.

'You're limping,' Dray Carlisle observed.

'It's okay,' she dismissed, although it clearly wasn't. A sharp pain was stabbing through the sole of her foot.

'You're also bleeding,' he added, and, halting her with a hand, called to his cousin, 'Carry on to the house, Si. We'll catch up.'

He supported her over to a fallen tree trunk. She sat while he examined her foot. He probed it gently but she still flinched.

'You can't walk on this. There's something embedded in it,' he declared, straightening up again.

Cass didn't see she had much choice and got to her feet. This time the pain was so excruciating she had to bite on her lip to stop from crying out.

'Full marks for stoicism,' Drayton Carlisle commented, 'none for common sense... Just hang on.'

He put an arm round her shoulders, the other behind her knees, and picked her up before she could voice a protest.

Cass was reduced to clasping her hands round his bare neck and looking anywhere but into the handsome face inches from hers.

His bare torso revealed toned muscle in a broad frame and carrying her was clearly no strain, yet she still felt a burden. Ultimately he was the one who had rescued the drowning child and now he had to rescue her and she'd barely said a pleasant word to him.

'I...um...thanks for what you did, Drayton,' she murmured inadequately. 'If you hadn't come along—'

'Someone else would have—and it's Dray.' He shrugged easily. 'Anyway, you're the brave one.'

'Me?' Cass didn't see it. 'Hardly. Stupid, maybe. I struggle to swim a length.'

'The whole point, surely,' he rejoined. 'You tried to save him despite being a poor swimmer.'

Cass wasn't having it. 'For all the good it did.'

'You were there. X marks the spot as it were,' he ran on. 'Without you, I would have been diving where the dinghy had drifted, downstream.'

Perhaps. Cass conceded that, and felt a little less foolish. It didn't change her view of events, however. He was the hero and an impressive one, too. Who would have thought it?

She stole a glance at his face and, reassessing, saw strength rather than arrogance in the masculine features. There was intelligence, too, as he caught her staring and read her mind with uncanny ease.

'So, do I get a second chance?'

To do what? Cass might have asked, but it seemed a rather leading question.

Instead she threw back, 'I didn't know you'd had a first one.'

He laughed—a deep laugh that made her aware of the mat of hair on his chest to which her hand had slipped. She moved it primly back to his shoulder.

'I thought I had and already blown it,' he admitted, 'when you abandoned me on the dance floor... Just as well I set off in pursuit.'

'You did?'

He nodded.

'After extricating myself. No sign of you, of course, just Si's son, William, in the throes of an asthma attack.'

'I didn't realise.' Cass recalled the first child wheezing but had been too concerned about the boy in danger to question why. 'Is he all right?'

'I imagine so.' Dray didn't seem too worried. 'William's attacks are more emotional than physical. I fetched his mother to take care of him while Simon and I investigated his garbled tale of a capsized dinghy and some woman in a blue dress who was going to take care of it.'

Only she hadn't and had come near to drowning alongside the other child, Cass realised.

'We should have raised the alarm, of course,' Dray added, 'but, at that point, we hadn't realised there was someone still in the river.'

'You came. That's the main thing.' She didn't hide her gratitude.

He slanted her a smile in return. 'The reward was worth it.'

Being with her, he meant, and Cass felt herself go warm under his gaze. She looked away again. She really couldn't cope with this man.

They passed the marquee, the reception still in full swing. Fortunately no one was around to see the bride's sister, half naked and looking like a drowned rat, in the arms of the groom's brother, also half naked but displaying a physique that merely enhanced *his* attraction.

They continued on up to the house where Simon's wife emerged from a French window to raise an elegant brow at the sight of them.

'Simon has called an ambulance,' she revealed. 'He's sent me to fetch the Stewarts. The boy's their son, apparently.'

Cass had met this woman briefly at the reception and had formed no impression at the time. Now she seemed a rather cold character.

'Well, be careful,' Dray advised in response. 'There's no need to panic them or disrupt the rest of the party. He's probably going to be all right.'

'Quite,' she agreed, 'although he's making a terrible fuss. He's been sick on one of your Persian carpets and now he's crying like a baby and—'

'Who's looking after him?' Dray cut into this less than sympathetic account.

'Mrs Henderson and Simon,' she informed him, before running on, 'I just hope no one is going to blame William for this. He's very shaken up. Apparently the Stewart child begged him to go out on the river, then deliberately rocked the—'

'Yes, all right, Camilla,' Dray interrupted once more, 'we can go into all this later. If you could fetch the Stewarts, I'd be grateful.'

If Camilla Carlisle looked a little miffed about being cut off mid-protest, she kept it to herself and walked off towards the marquee.

Cass was left agog at her self-centredness.

'Did you believe that?' she demanded on a slightly indignant note.

'Do I look stupid?' Dray drawled back.

Cass supposed not. But if he'd known William or Camilla was lying, why had he accepted it?

'It didn't seem a particularly appropriate time to give Camilla the third degree,' he answered her unspoken question, 'but don't worry, I promise to dust off the thumbscrews later.'

'Very funny.' Cass pulled a face and wished he hadn't such an uncanny knack of reading her mind. 'You can put me down now,' she added as they entered the house but, if he heard, he chose to ignore.

Instead he continued along a corridor until they reached a bathroom. He set her down on the toilet seat, then soaked a towel under warm water before proceeding to kneel beside her and wipe the dirt from her injured foot.

He took time and care and Cass lost the will to argue as she became conscious of his touch. It was a powerful combination, gentleness and strength. He turned over her foot and cleaned the sole, before re-examining her injury.

'The bleeding's slowed,' he murmured, 'but I definitely think there's something in the cut. Best left to the professionals, I suspect... Meanwhile a little antiseptic would not go amiss.'

He reached for a bottle out of the medicine cabinet.

Cass watched him pour a liberal amount onto a cotton-wool pad and gritted her teeth in readiness, knowing it was going to sting.

'Swear if you want,' he suggested as he dabbed between her flinches.

'Don't tempt me.' She shut her eyes until he ceased his ministrations and the pain subsided.

'I wish I could.' He was now seated on the edge of the bath, and, catching her slightly startled gaze, added, 'So what does it take?'

To tempt her?

Could he really be interested? It seemed unlikely. She must look a sorry mess, yet he was definitely flirting.

She decided to go for silent disdain. She almost managed it, but her blush was a bit of a give-away. The trouble was she *did* find him attractive. Very.

He smiled at her, slow and amused, as if he knew how she felt and she threw his earlier words back at him, 'Do *I* look stupid?'

'Would you have to be?'

'I think so, don't you?'

They'd returned to sparring but it was only superficial. The undercurrent was something else entirely.

'Is this a money or a class thing?' he guessed astutely. 'Because I have no problem with you being a checkout girl.'

'That's big of you.' Her tone was strictly ironic as she decided he desperately needed cutting down to size. 'Could be a *I just don't fancy you* thing?'

'I suppose.' The man seemed impervious to insult. 'Let's see, shall we?'

Still smiling, he stood up and lifted her back into his arms. Caught by surprise, she clutched at broad shoulders. And just like that, he kissed her.

She was always to remember that first time. His lips were warm and hard, and he smelled of a blend of sweat and river and cologne that was wholly masculine. When she pushed at his chest, her fingers meshed with damp body hair and her heart kicked up a beat. She made some sound, half protest, half moan. He took it for acquiescence and perhaps it was, the struggle was so brief. A clash of teeth before she opened her lips, a deep shudder going through her when he began to probe the sweet wet cavern of her mouth, then the thrust of tongues as her hand finally snaked round his neck to hold his head to hers.

Her response was all a man could have hoped for and more—but Dray was quite unprepared. One kiss and he found he'd never wanted any woman so badly. He had the urge to take her right then and there, to lay her down onto the tiled floor, to touch the warm willing body in his arms and cover it with his.

The blood was rushing to Cass's head, pounding through her veins, and she grasped handfuls of his hair as they began to bite and play with each other's mouths. She wanted, *needed* more. It was like the passion in poems and songs— the earth was moving and she didn't care that it was Drayton Carlisle who was doing it for her.

He was the one who finally broke off the kiss, forced to as she slipped in his arms and they almost overbalanced. He saved them both but, in doing so, knocked her injured foot against the wall.

Cass was left gasping aloud with pain. It was some reality check!

'I'm sorry.' Dray's tone was contrite but his expression wasn't remotely so.

'Well, you don't look it,' accused Cass, rapidly recovering her sanity.

'Sorry, it's just... Who'd have thought it?'

If Cass had been a fool, she would have said, *Thought what?* But she wasn't. She knew full well what he meant. Who would have thought that she could be so passionate?

It had come as something of a surprise to Cass, too.

'It doesn't prove anything,' she said, as much for her own benefit as his.

'No,' he seemed to agree with her.

But Cass didn't want him to. She wanted the battle to recommence so they could discount what had happened.

'So if you've finished playing *macho man*—' she took refuge in sarcasm '—I'd like to find a phone and call a taxi.'

'To take you where exactly?'

'The railway station.'

'Right.' He glanced downwards and his gaze lingered long enough to make Cass snatch the sides of her shirt together, belatedly concealing the swell of her breasts. 'Well, that should help boost rail travel, at least.'

The dry comment reminded Cass she was in no state to stand on her dignity—no state to stand, full stop—but it didn't stop her wriggling in his arms.

'Okay, I'm walking,' he added quickly and, hooking the door with his foot, strode back along the corridor until they reached the main living room.

There the rescued boy lay on a sofa, attended to by his parents and Dray's housekeeper. He was pale and tearful but clearly on the road to recovery.

Dray deposited Cass on an armchair before pulling on a fine wool jumper produced by the housekeeper. Cass happily faded into the background, leaving him to field questions from the boy's parents. They knew the bare facts but wanted the full story.

Cass coloured as she listened to his version where she was the heroine responsible for saving their child. Simon Carlisle might have disputed it but he seemed to have disappeared somewhere and Cass didn't get the chance before the ambulance arrived.

The paramedics were reassuring but decided to take the boy to hospital as a precaution. They would have taken Cass, too, only they agreed with Dray that a GP could treat her foot and without the inevitable wait in Casualty on a busy Saturday afternoon.

Cass wasn't given any say in the matter.

As the ambulance men and the Stewart family departed, Simon Carlisle reappeared, showered and in a fresh shirt.

Dray asked how his son was and the other man made a slight face before relaying that William was fine but had been taken home by his mother. He had stayed on in case his help was needed.

Dray nodded and asked his cousin to return to the reception and ensure everything was going smoothly. He then dispatched his housekeeper to run a bath.

'I don't need a bath!' Cass protested somewhat ridiculously when he picked her up in his arms once more.

'Really?' He sniffed the air, as they walked towards the staircase. 'Ah! Let me guess. *Eau de* Thames, a subtle blend of sewage, old car tyres and toxic chemicals.'

Cass didn't have to pretend offence. 'And I suppose you imagine you still smell of Rico Sabine.'

'Ted Charles,' he told her his normal choice of cologne. 'Just in case we end up on Christmas present terms.'

There he was, flirting again, and Cass didn't know how to

handle it. Flirting back didn't seem a wise move. They'd already reached the kissing stage without the slightest encouragement from her.

'What did you give the man who has everything?' she finally quipped back. 'A wide berth!'

He made a face, as if crestfallen. 'So what have you against us rich folk?' he asked, very much tongue-in-cheek.

'Where to begin?' she replied. 'Ignorance, insensitivity, greed...'

'Not to mention war, famine and death,' he cut in dryly. 'They're probably all down to us, too.'

'Probably,' Cass echoed, 'but I think it's their arrogance I find most unbearable.'

'Speaking *im*personally, of course.'

'Of course.'

But they both knew it had been a dig at him. He just wasn't bothered. That was real arrogance for you.

The conversation was curtailed as they reached the first floor and he carried her through a bedroom to the bathroom beyond. There they found his housekeeper pouring a liberal amount of essence in a piping hot bath.

Cass wondered if the whole world had noticed she was less than fragrant.

The housekeeper scuttled out of the room on their arrival. Perhaps she imagined they wanted privacy.

Cass didn't. She remembered what had happened in the downstairs bathroom and she wasn't ready for an encore.

He set her down on a wicker chair. She sat primly, waiting for him to leave.

'Towels, soap, shampoo, bathrobe.' He checked each item off. 'Anything else you need?'

'No.'

'Sure?'

'Yes.'

'Back wash, maybe?'

Cass's eyes widened in alarm, before she caught the amused look on his face.

'No, thank you,' she muttered heavily.

'Shame.' He smiled, already backing out of the door.

Cass told herself to get a grip. Sure he might fancy her, but it didn't mean he was going to pounce on her, uninvited.

She took her time in washing—her foot hardly allowed her to do otherwise—and it was almost an hour before she emerged, wrapped in the folds of a towelling robe, to find the housekeeper in the bedroom beyond.

The older woman smiled before announcing, 'The doctor is outside.'

'Doctor?' quizzed Cass.

'Dr Michaelson. Mr Dray called him. Should I show him in?'

'Yes, all right.'

Cass wasn't about to argue. If she did, she suspected more than the doctor would materialise.

'Sorry about this,' she murmured as a youngish man dressed in a smart suit entered the room. 'I hope I haven't spoiled your day.'

'Not at all—' he indicated that she should sit on the bed '—quite the contrary, in fact. I was knee-deep in dirty shirts when I got the call.'

Cass eyed him quizzically.

He laughed, 'No, I don't normally do my laundry in a suit and tie. Dray suggested I join the reception. After I've killed or cured you, of course.'

She smiled a little, before asking, 'You're friends?'

'Sort of,' he responded. 'I act as Medical Officer at Carlisle Electronics one day a week... The name's John, by the way.'

'John, right.' Cass winced as he probed the wound.

'Nasty cut,' he mused aloud.

'I think it's glass,' she volunteered in turn.

'Looks like,' he agreed. 'Well, we have a choice—we can do this the easy way or the hard way.'

'Which are?'

'I can try to locate said glass while you grit your teeth and bear it—'

'Or?'

'I can inject a walloping great dose of anaesthetic into your foot, wait till it's completely dead, then cut deeply enough to ensure all foreign bodies are expelled.'

Cass raised a brow at this information. 'And the easy one is?'

He laughed. 'Quite.'

'How long will the walloping dose last?'

'Depends. A good few hours, at least. You'll be blissfully pain-free.'

'But immobile?'

He gave another nod and waited while Cass debated her choice.

'I think the walloping dose, don't you?' a third voice drawled.

Cass looked over the doctor's shoulder to find Dray Carlisle, dressed once more in pristine white shirt, tie, waist-coat and trousers, watching from the door left wide open by the housekeeper. How long had he been there? And why hadn't he announced his presence earlier?

'I'd like to try the other method first,' she stated categor-ically.

Dray gave her a look that questioned if she was being purposely difficult, while the young doctor awaited further instruction.

'And *I'm* the patient,' Cass reminded them both.

'Of course.' John Michaelson began to rummage in his medical bag.

Dray didn't pursue the argument, but settled for glaring at her from the doorway.

Cass really didn't want a dead foot for hours on end so she gritted her teeth as suggested and gripped the edge of the bed and somehow stopped herself from screaming aloud, but it was all to no avail. The glass was embedded too deeply. She wasn't going to call a halt, however.

The sweat was standing out in beads on her forehead when Dray finally did it for her. 'For God's sake, John, give her the injection! Can't you see she's in pain?'

His voice was gruff, angry even, but John Michaelson didn't seem to take exception. He stopped immediately and raised his eyes to Cass's face.

'He may be right. I can see the glass but I'll need to cut deeper to reach it.'

'Okay, do what you think is best.'

Resigned, Cass watched him prepare the injection, then looked towards the door as he administered it.

She half expected to see a triumphant look on Dray Carlisle's face. He'd won, after all—laid down the law.

But his face was expressionless, except for a nerve pulsing at his temple, and the next moment he was gone, footsteps retreating down the corridor.

'He's just concerned,' John Michaelson said, catching her frown.

She quickly blanked off expression. 'Doesn't bother me. Let him throw a moody, if he likes.'

Her words surprised, then amused the other man. 'Drayton Carlisle throwing a moody—an interesting concept... Are *you* friends?' he echoed her earlier question.

Only he gave it a different twist—friends as in lovers. Or was she being over-sensitive?

'I hardly know the man, actually,' she said with some conviction.

She really didn't. One moment he was the urbane charmer, the next a complete autocrat.

'Still have feeling?' John Michaelson enquired and for a

mad second she thought they were on the same subject. Then she noticed he was pressing the blade of the scalpel to the sole of her foot.

'Nothing,' she replied, and was careful to remain immobile as he extracted a wicked-looking shard of glass, before cleaning and dressing the wound.

He stayed to talk a while but the conversation made little impression on Cass.

Her head was still full of Dray Carlisle.

Her heart, too, if truth be told, only she hadn't quite admitted it then.

CHAPTER FOUR

THREE years on Cass returned to a very different present, alerted by the sound of approaching footsteps.

She turned, expecting to see Tom, and her back stiffened at the sight of his older brother, towering above her. He'd removed his jacket but left on his black tie.

He studied her face for a moment and Cass was glad she'd hidden her eyes behind sunglasses. She didn't want him to know she'd been crying.

She got to her feet, ignoring his offer of a hand up, and brushed dust from the back of her skirt before asking, 'Where's Tom?'

'Up at the house,' he told her. 'He won't come down here.'

Or big brother wouldn't let him?

'Fine.' She checked her watch and discovered it was past twelve. 'Well, if he wants to speak to me, he knows where I live.'

She folded her jacket over her arm and took him by surprise as she walked away. She got as far as the copse of trees before a hand restrained her.

'Look, he's not playing games with you, if that's what you think. It's just the summer house... It has unhappy associations for him.'

The latter admission was slow in coming, so slow Cass felt he was making it up as he went along.

'What associations?' she asked in disbelief.

She wanted to see how good his powers of invention were. Not very, it seemed.

'It's not important,' he dismissed.

Cass sensed he was hiding something—if only his feelings.

His tone was clipped and precise yet the pulse at his temple was beating in overdrive, and his eyes held disdain. He disliked her as much as she did him.

'Neither's meeting Tom for me,' she stated and tried to slip from his grip.

His fingers tightened automatically. 'All right. If I tell you the truth, you'll come to the house?'

Cass wondered if she had any choice. He was stronger, bigger and suddenly a little frightening in his intensity.

She nodded slowly, then wished she hadn't as he resumed, 'Your sister used to meet one of her lovers in the summer house. Tom found out about it.'

Cass's throat closed up and she swallowed hard, but she still hadn't a thing to say. She wanted to call him a liar only she couldn't find the conviction.

Her silence spoke volumes to Dray. 'You already knew this, didn't you?'

'No!' That she could deny.

'But it isn't a total shock to you,' he pursued.

Cass shook her head. She was aware of the affair, just not the details.

'Did *you* know?' she challenged in return. 'Was it you who told Tom?'

'No, on both counts. *Tom* told *me* but he was scarcely coherent. I didn't quite believe it till now. It's true, though, isn't it?'

'I'm not sure.'

'Yes, you are.' Anger now narrowed those unusually dark blue eyes. 'You might not have been close but the one thing I know you and your sister discussed was your sex lives.'

Cass's lips parted in mute protest. Pen might have occasionally been indiscreet, but Cass had never reciprocated. She'd always regarded such matters as private.

'I wouldn't bother with that innocent look,' he grated on,

'because she told me as much. She said how you rated us. Men, that is. *All* your men.'

'My men?' Cass was struggling to catch up.

'That's something else she told me—what a busy *social* life you had.' His mouth curved into a bitter smile. 'So what benchmark do you use? Technique? Stamina? Or something more quantifiable like orgasms per night?'

Cass shook her head, finally finding the voice to accuse, 'You're making this up. Pen wouldn't say anything like that.'

'Oh, wouldn't she?' He gave a hollow laugh.

Cass had a moment's doubt. But no. Why should Pen tell lies about her?

'Of course, you don't actually, do you?' he went on—inexorably, degradingly on. 'Rate us, I mean. Not in any real sense. We're nobody. Just there to give Cassandra Barker a good, hard—'

'*Don't!*' She cut off the profanity before it could be uttered, and almost jerked free of him.

He grabbed her back. 'What's the matter? I thought you northerners appreciated plain speaking.'

'You and I—it wasn't like that! You know it wasn't!' A welter of emotions rose to the surface.

'I *thought* it wasn't,' he sneered back, 'but then I was suffering from a brain bypass at the time. Thank God your little sister put me straight.'

Cass heard the rancour in his voice, but still refused to believe a word.

'I'm not listening to this!' she tried to shout him down.

'Oh, you'll listen—' he yanked her closer '—you'll listen as long as I want you to listen.'

'Like hell I will!' Railing against his arrogance, she struggled once more, only this time, when he wouldn't release her, she kicked him hard on the shin.

He swore aloud, more in surprise than pain, and Cass wasn't given the chance to repeat the assault.

She found herself backed hard against the nearest tree, arms twisted round the trunk, feet barely touching the ground.

'Let me go!' Green eyes sparked with rage as she tried and failed to land another kick.

Dray held her fast until she gave up fighting and took to staring past him with tight-lipped fury. He hadn't meant things to get physical but he had forgotten she had a temper.

The rest he remembered now she was close enough for her breasts to rise and fall against his chest, close enough to feel her breath on his face, to smell the unique scent of her. The trouble was he remembered it all too vividly: how real it had felt when they'd made love, how perfectly her body had moved to the rhythm of his, how badly he'd needed to possess her. He remembered, also, what a fool he'd been, talking of love, when it had just been sex...was still sex.

Cass's breathing shallowed to a whisper as she became aware of him watching her.

He released one of her arms but only so he could cup her face with a hand. He turned her gaze to his and wouldn't let her look away. Ice-blue eyes somehow burned a path to her heart, making it hurt.

'Tell me how it was, then, Cass,' he finally murmured, 'you and I.'

'I—I—' Cass didn't know any more. She'd forgotten why they were arguing, forgotten why they were here.

The years were falling away and once more she was in the grip of an emotion so powerful it blanked out reason.

It was a living force, invading her body, as hands went round her waist and drew her to him. It was a sickness, spreading through her, as, unerringly, his mouth sought hers, and, helplessly, her lips parted. It was a drug, rushing through her veins, straight to her heart and head.

No words were spoken. Words were irrelevant. Need was all. The need to touch, be touched. To re-affirm life on a day shadowed by death.

Or maybe it was just sex. Raw and immediate, as he lifted her against the cool rough bark, mouth still kissing, hard, passionate, close to violent in its intent. Then it was hands, pulling at her blouse, almost tearing, stripping bare, flesh swelling, aching for his teeth, his tongue. It was that other Cass, gasping, moaning, clinging to him as desire flowed through her like a river.

His mouth was at her breast, his hand already pushing between her thighs when they were thrown an unwanted lifeline, one that couldn't be ignored: a voice calling, far away at first, but homing in on them.

Any earlier and they would have been saved their brief insanity.

Later and they would have been making love on the ground.

As it was, Dray Carlisle stopped only when the voice came dangerously near and she started to push him away in panic.

'It's okay.' He released her slowly. 'It's my Personal Assistant, Alec Stewart.'

Alec Stewart—the father of the boy they'd rescued all that time ago.

But why was that okay? Cass wondered as she desperately smoothed her skirt back down and tried to redo buttons, finding she had two extra thumbs.

He brushed her hands away and she submitted to him fastening what he'd earlier almost ripped apart.

The answer came to her: of course it was okay for him! He was the rich, powerful Drayton Carlisle. Ordinary rules didn't apply to him. He could do what he liked.

She was just the pathetic piece who let him—and on the day of her sister's funeral.

Shame hit her in a wave. She couldn't look at him so she looked at the ground until he was finished, then, picking up her fallen jacket, she walked unsteadily away as Alec Stewart approached.

She had no idea where she was going. She was just desperate to get away, asking herself over and over: how could she? On today of all days, how could she allow him—of all people—to make love to her?

Perhaps he was right. She was oversexed.

But could that be? Over the past three years she'd had one single brief relationship.

No, it was him. He just had to touch her and she turned into slut of the year. It had been the same the last time.

Only the last time she'd dressed it up as love and dreamed of happy-ever-afters...

She rewound once more, back to Pen's wedding day and let the tape play on.

The young doctor had left and she'd lain where she was. She'd been so tired, her abortive rescue bid coming on top of a sleepless night. She'd shut her eyes for a moment and the next, had been fast asleep

She'd been woken by a gentle hand. Dray Carlisle had been standing by the bed.

'Your sister will be going soon. Do you feel up to coming down?'

She stared up at him, slowly recalling the day's events until she reached the most momentous—their kiss. The rest—weddings and rescues and injured feet—meant little in comparison.

'Are you all right?' he added at her silence.

'Yes...Yes, of course.'

'I've borrowed some clothes for you.'

He indicated a dress and underwear lying at the foot of the large bed.

'Thanks.'

'I'll wait outside.'

He left, shutting the door quietly behind him. He no longer seemed angry with her, just remote.

Blinking away sleep, Cass glanced at her watch and discovered she'd lost almost three hours.

She sat up and shuffled to the borrowed clothes. The bra was too small but she slipped on lacy white pants that looked as if they'd never been worn. The dress was mint-green and sleeveless, bearing an expensive label, and Cass wondered whose it was. It felt tight round the bust and was a little short in the leg but otherwise fitted. In the absence of any make-up, she settled for combing her long hair loose.

She was more or less ready when he returned, knocking first before entering.

They traded stares once more.

Cass realised she was never going to get used to him being this handsome.

His gaze was intense but his face unreadable.

She pushed herself up from the bed and almost instantly sat back down. She was unable to feel her foot but had thought by some miracle it would actually do its job and support her.

'I'll carry you down,' he said matter-of-factly.

'Yes, all right.' She didn't want to make a fuss. Making a fuss would be tantamount to admitting that it affected her, being close to him.

'Unless you'd prefer John,' he added, sensing her reluctance.

'John?'

'Dr Michaelson.'

Cass pulled a slight face, saying, 'I wouldn't think carrying patients is quite in his job description.'

'He might make an exception in your case,' Dray suggested. 'He seemed somewhat smitten.'

'Smitten?' The archaic term almost made her laugh.

Would have made her laugh only he clearly wasn't joking.

'Perhaps I'm wrong and his interest in where you live and what you do—' he arched a brow '—is purely medical.'

'I bet you couldn't resist telling him I'm a checkout girl,' she accused in reply.

'As a matter of fact, I told him nothing.'

'Oh.'

Cass felt wrong-footed as well as dead-footed as he at last crossed to her side and, placing one arm under her shoulders, the other at her knees, lifted her up from the bed.

Only when they were walking from the room did he add, 'Nothing apart from what should be obvious.'

Cass knew she shouldn't ask but couldn't resist. 'And that is?'

'His interest wasn't welcome.'

'Right.'

But it wasn't right. How did *he* know whether it was welcome or not?

'So you feel you can speak for me?' she challenged and made the mistake of looking straight at him.

He looked straight back as he replied, 'I was speaking for myself.'

Cass's *Oh* this time was barely mouthed as she realised from the set of his face that they were no longer playing games—if they ever had been.

He didn't say more, didn't need to. It was in his eyes, in the way he held her.

He wanted her.

And she…?

Laid her head against his shoulder, trying to hide away her own feelings, and trembled as he buried his face in her hair.

Wanted him, too.

It seemed that simple as he continued down the long staircase and out to the terrace and across summer lawns, holding her close, touching but not kissing, intimate in their own time and place.

Then they entered the marquee and the spell was broken

by the heat and the noise and, most especially, her sister's face as they approached.

Annoyance was quickly masked as Dray set Cass down at the table and various people congratulated Cass on that afternoon's rescue, but when Dray went with Tom to fetch drinks, Pen launched into a full inquisition.

She'd heard the rescue story, of course, but hadn't quite believed it. She knew Cass was a poor swimmer.

Cass was honest, giving credit where credit was due, and stuck to the facts, but there must have been something in her voice, a different tone when she used Dray's name.

Pen homed into it straight away. 'What's going on?' she hissed under cover of the music.

'I just told you.'

'Not that. You and Dray?'

'What?'

Were her feelings so obvious?

'Don't play the innocent,' Pen continued. 'Every half an hour he's been up to the house, checking how you are.'

So she hadn't been forgotten! Cass struggled to hide her pleasure in the fact.

'I was asleep,' she said in her defence.

'Really? You'd think you were at death's door the way he's carrying on.' Pen's tone was so sharp no one could miss the jealousy in it.

Over Dray? The thought slipped into Cass's mind but she pushed it out again. It was attention being focused on Cass, that was all. Understandable, surely, when it was Pen's big day.

'Look, I'm sorry if it's spoiled things a little for you—' Cass took her sister's hand and squeezed it, wanting to make up with her '—and, of course, you're right, it's a fuss about nothing. Chances are he's simply in a sweat, worrying that I'll sue him for negligence.'

Pen was still frowning but looked ready to be convinced. 'How could you do that?'

'Unfenced river banks? Dangerous glass left lying around?' Both reasons sounded improbable but it was the best Cass could do off the cuff.

Pen was happy enough with them, although she quickly moved to panic. 'You wouldn't really sue him, would you? You can't! You might think they're a bunch of snobs, who deserve what they get, but I have to live with this family.'

'God, Pen, calm down!' Cass couldn't believe her sister sometimes. 'Ask yourself, am I likely to go home tonight and call our lawyer?'

'We haven't got a lawyer.'

'Exactly.'

The Carlisles probably had a firm of them, primed at any time to do battle.

'Anyway, I just want to forget the whole stupid incident,' Cass concluded, 'and I hope you will, too.'

Pen looked slightly mollified and managed to switch a smile back on as Tom returned, closely followed by Dray.

If talking to Pen had brought Cass back to the real world, meeting Dray's gaze had her head in clouds once more. Only now they had an audience and it was like being drunk when it was important to seem sober.

She tore her eyes away and kept them fixed on anyone and anything rather than him, and concentrated on making normal-sounding responses to Tom and Pen before they took their leave of the wedding party.

Dray and other friends and family accompanied them up to the terrace where a chauffeured car waited to take them the thirty miles to London and their first honeymoon night at the Ritz.

Cass was left once more with Uncle Charles. She tried hard to focus on what the older man was saying but her head seemed to be in a fog. She drank down a glass of champagne, then another. Hardly guaranteed to clear her head. Perhaps she didn't want to.

The music played on and couples danced and Cass waited. Dray returned and sat down beside her and, without a word, took her hand in his.

There were other people at the table—his cousin Simon, his uncle, family friends. He didn't seem to care who saw them.

It was Cass who said very quietly, 'We can't do this,' even as her heart turned over.

'Yes, we can,' he replied and went on holding her hand.

They didn't talk much. For once in her life Cass was nervous. She sipped at her drink and listened as he conversed with the others.

The party was in its dying stages when he finally left his cousin and uncle to wind things down and carried Cass back to the house. Her foot was pain-free but dead. There was no discussion as to how she was going to get home. He assumed she'd stay.

She assumed it, too.

He took her to the room where earlier she'd slept. He bypassed the bed and went through to the bathroom.

'I thought you'd like a wash.'

'Yes, fine.'

He sat her on a wooden linen box next to the sink and took down from a cabinet toothpaste and a spare toothbrush.

Cass washed her face while he went through to the bedroom and returned with the bathrobe.

'Are you going to manage?'

'Yes. Yes, of course.'

'If you undress, I'll come back in ten minutes to carry you to bed. All right?'

Cass nodded and managed to hide her feelings until he left. She'd imagined him carrying her upstairs and seducing her. She'd guessed at her own reaction, a mixture of dread and desire. What she hadn't anticipated was this sudden detachment. It made her feel let down and foolish and more heart-sore than she'd have believed possible.

She concentrated on getting ready for bed, levering herself on and off the toilet, using the edge of the sink for balance as she stripped off clothes and put on the white bathrobe. She wrapped it round her body tight and adopted a closed-down expression on his return.

He carried her to the bed and set her down on the edge where he'd pulled back the duvet. She shuffled into a sitting position against the pillows and, keeping the robe on, dragged the cover over her legs.

'I'll say goodnight, then.' He stepped back from the bed.

'Goodnight.' She studied the bedcover.

Her tone was abrupt and Dray realised his own remoteness had caused it. He'd been trying to do the right thing, but now wondered what that was. He gazed at her until she raised her eyes back to his.

Compelled to look at him, Cass felt the truth finally dawn on her. His desire for her hadn't died or diminished. It was just being rigidly controlled.

'If I kiss you,' he told her quietly, 'I won't want to stop. In fact, I might not be able to. You understand?'

'Yes.'

'And I don't think you're quite ready for that,' he added without rancour, 'so I'd prefer to wait until you are.'

Cass agreed. She wasn't ready for him and was never going to be. He was too everything. Handsome, smart, sexy, rich. And she was hardly enough—a passing pretty, small town girl.

But if he waited, it wouldn't happen. Tomorrow they'd waken up to the real world and recognise how impossible they were together.

No, this was their moment in time.

She watched him walk to the door and turn to ask, 'Shall I put out the light?'

She nodded, and said under cover of darkness, 'I'd like you to kiss me, too.'

It was greeted with total silence. She held her breath and time seemed to stand still. Then the door clicked shut behind him.

Cass had a moment's anguish, thinking he had gone, before she heard the sound of footfalls on the soft carpeting.

He sat on the edge of the bed. It was too dark to catch his eyes or read his face now but there was infinite tenderness in his voice as he said, 'Are you sure?'

'Y-yes.'

'You don't sound it.'

'I am... But if you've changed your mind—'

'Silly girl,' he cut in gently and gathered her into his arms. He kissed her and, just as he'd said, couldn't stop.

But Cass hadn't wanted him to. Even now, years later, she didn't pretend otherwise. They had made love that very first time but it had been far from the last. For three long wonderful weeks, he'd wined and dined her and taken her to the theatre and brought her home at weekends. They'd laughed together and talked of anything and everything and made love every chance they had got until Cass had almost believed it wasn't so impossible, the shop-girl and the tycoon.

It had all ended in tears, of course. *Her* tears. Tom and Pen had returned from honeymoon and suddenly it had been over.

No explanation. He'd dumped her as quickly as he'd picked her up.

Pen had tried to make her feel better. It wasn't personal to Cass. Dray always operated that way. What he wanted, he got—then lost interest in having it.

It had been no consolation, however, knowing she'd been

one in a long line, realising how easily she'd fallen for his looks and charm.

But pride had reasserted itself. Too late to stop her behaving foolishly, but in time for her to get her life back on track. He'd treated her as if she were nobody, so she had resolved to become somebody. Not in his terms, perhaps, but in hers, as she'd returned to university to complete her degree.

Now here she was, a junior doctor, and it seemed nothing had changed. He still took. She still let him. Being the day of her sister's funeral hadn't stopped them. Nor the awful things he'd said about her, made worse by his attributing them to Pen.

He still took and she still let and, if the past had taught her anything, it was to run this time, to run as fast and as far as she could from Drayton Carlisle.

CHAPTER FIVE

ONLY running was hard through tangled undergrowth and fallen trees, and she hadn't really any idea where she was any more.

She sped up a little when she heard her name being called and footsteps tracking behind, but it was no good. Instead of coming out onto lawn, she came up against the barrier of a wooden fence and realised she'd reached the edge of Carlisle property.

She had brief thoughts of hitching her skirt up and climbing over before common sense prevailed. Who knew what lay on the other side—a pack of guard dogs, a rifle-toting landowner?

Dray Carlisle appeared shortly thereafter to state the obvious. 'You're a little lost.'

She glanced at him briefly. He was cool and composed, as ever; it might have been a different man who'd been making love to her moments ago.

'The house is this way.' He indicated the path he'd come and waited for her to go ahead of him.

Cass didn't see she had much choice.

She followed the well-beaten track until the wood turned into scrub grass, then lawn. They walked towards the house in silence but he stopped her before she could climb the steps to the terrace.

'About what happened down at the river—' he began in measured tones.

'You were lying, weren't you?' she cut in before he could say more.

'Lying?'

'About Pen telling you those things.'

Cass waited for an answer but he seemed in no hurry to give one, his eyes speculative. She regretted asking.

'Don't bother,' she quelled any doubts. 'I know you were.'

'I shouldn't have said anything,' he finally returned. 'Not today, anyway.'

Cass read it as an admission of guilt and was satisfied.

It was Dray who continued, 'I shouldn't have kissed you either.'

'Forget it,' she threw back. 'I have.'

'That easy, is it?' His mouth twisted in a parody of a smile.

No, it wasn't *that bloody easy*, but Cass saw a way to hit back.

'Frankly, yes,' she agreed coldly and actually enjoyed the look on his face. If he'd imagined he was anyone special, he didn't now.

'Well, as long as you talk to Tom,' he responded at length, making it clear his brother was still his priority.

Cass said nothing, taking the steps to the terrace. She wanted to get away altogether but Tom, who had been looking out for them, emerged from a doorway and came towards them.

'I couldn't go down there,' he said without preamble. 'Not to the summer house. You understand?'

Cass nodded. 'I think so.'

'She used to use it. I found out,' he ran on. 'The floor, I suppose. There isn't a settee... Or the chair, maybe. Did she tell you?'

Cass stared back at him, speechless. Was this all he wanted to ask her?

She mouthed something at Dray Carlisle and then walked away once more.

He caught her up, grabbing her arm.

She rounded on him furiously, 'Didn't you catch that? Well, it was *naff off*. Is that clear enough?'

'Calm down,' he instructed, glancing back at an agitated Tom. 'I didn't know he was going to ask you something like that.'

'I bet!' she spat at him, 'Well, just for the record, let me tell you: I don't know anything about the affair she had; I don't know his name, what age he is, where he lives, how good he is in bed. Nothing! And I don't want to know.'

'Yes, okay. Fair enough.' He signalled for her to hush and attempted to pacify her with, 'I believe you.'

'No, you don't!' she snapped at this patent insincerity. 'But it's true all the same. I've seen my sister half a dozen times in the last three years and on none of these occasions did we trade bedroom secrets. All right?' Her voice rose with her temper but he still didn't respond in kind.

Instead he looked hard at her, then towards the house.

Finally Cass noticed the set of French doors just feet away. They were open to let in air on this warm day. Beyond them was the drawing room where people were eating their buffet lunch—or had been until they'd heard angry voices and stopped to gaze out onto the terrace.

'Oh, God!' Cass looked aghast as she tried to remember what she'd said. 'Do you think they heard?'

'Probably.' He didn't go out of his way to make her feel any better. 'I think I'd better rejoin the funeral party and defuse the situation.'

'You don't expect me to go in there, too.' Cass didn't know these people, didn't want to.

Dray shook his head. 'I gave up *expecting anything* from you a long time ago, Cassie,' he said with a sudden weariness. 'You can go now, if you want. Perhaps it's best.'

Go? Now he'd turned her world upside down again. Go? Now he had no more use for her. Nothing really had changed.

'She can't go,' came from Tom listening on the sidelines. 'Dray, she can't go. I don't know what to do… Cass, please. You have to help me…'

He fixed desperate eyes on her, clearly at the end of his tether.

Cass could walk away on Dray Carlisle; she owed him nothing. But Tom was different.

'It's all right, Tom, I'll stay,' she replied quietly.

'Thank you.' He shut his eyes in momentary relief. 'It has to be a secret. We'll go somewhere...'

'My sitting room,' Dray suggested and Tom nodded, turning to lead the way.

Cass made to follow but Dray caught her arm once more. 'I'll be as quick as I can. Don't take anything Tom says too seriously,' he instructed in an undertone. 'He's...he's not himself.'

'I realise that.' Cass wondered if he thought her a fool on top of everything else. 'Don't worry. I'll just let him talk.'

'Good.' He let her go but she could feel his eyes boring into her back as she walked away with Tom.

Tom took her down a long corridor to a room used exclusively by the family. It was walled by battered bookcases and furnished with an old chesterfield sofa and easy chairs round an Adam fireplace. No interior designer had been let loose in here and it was the more relaxing for it.

The fire wasn't lit, of course. It was too warm.

She refused Tom's offer of whisky and watched in concern as he clinked the crystal decanter against a glass and poured himself what was at least a double measure.

He drank it down, then refilled the glass, bringing it with him as he sank down on a sofa. She sat in a seat opposite.

She waited for him to speak but, now that they were alone, he seemed to be having difficulty finding words.

'You knew her, didn't you,' he choked out at last, 'better than anyone?'

Cass could have said yes, but was that what he wanted to hear?

'I wouldn't say that,' she hedged.

'But you knew about the baby?' Blue eyes suddenly focused on her.

She shook her head. 'Actually, no, I didn't. Not until this week... How is she?' she added quietly.

He frowned, then dismissed impatiently, 'I didn't mean that baby. I meant the other one.'

Cass felt her stomach drop. She should have been expecting it, of course.

'The other one?' She played for time.

'She had a baby before.' His mouth twisted with pain. 'The doctors assumed I knew... *You* must have.'

Cass couldn't see a way of denying it and there was no reason to, any more. Pen was dead.

'Yes, Pen had a baby when she was younger,' she confirmed quietly.

'How much younger?'

'Does that matter?'

'Yes, it bloody matters!'

Angry, he sounded more like his big brother, but Cass forgave him it. His whole world had fallen apart a week ago.

'She was sixteen.'

'Whose was it?'

'A boy she met at a party. He wasn't much older.'

'She must have liked him,' Tom considered, 'to have had the baby.'

'I suppose.' Cass decided against telling him that it had been too late for Pen to do anything else. 'She *was* very young, Tom. It was a mistake. She wanted to forget all about it. You can understand that.'

She spoke gently but Tom resented it all the same. He didn't want to understand Pen. He wanted to hurt her for all the lies she'd told him, only she was out of reach.

Cass was the next best thing, as he threw at her, 'And where were you when this was all happening? Too busy with your own life to bother keeping an eye on her?'

Cass blanched at the accusation, accepting there might be some truth in it. She had been immersed in her studies at the time Pen had gone off the rails.

'I…I'm sorry.' Tom sensed the hurt in her silence and was concerned she might leave. 'I shouldn't have said that. I have no quarrel with you.'

'It's all right.' Cass realised it had been his grief talking.

'But I need to know,' he continued raggedly, 'what happened to it—Pen's first baby?'

She kept her emotions in check as she relayed, 'He died shortly after birth.'

It was a very long time since she'd talked of this. In fact, Cass and Pen had almost never talked of it. Alexander Joseph, born two months early, had barely drawn a breath. Despite an initial reluctance to accept her pregnancy, Pen had been devastated by the loss.

'I'd assumed he'd been adopted.'

'That had been discussed.'

'It's not hard, is it? To find them a family, I mean. Lots of couples desperate for a baby.'

'I imagine not.'

Even as she said the words, Cass felt they were wrong. It was hard. To carry that small body and feel the slight beat of its heart against yours. To stroke the down on its head, the soft curve of its cheek. To do all that, then hand it over, like a parcel sent to an incorrect address. Hard? It must be killing.

'Best solution all round.' Tom was on his own train of thought. 'Don't you think?'

This time Cass said nothing. She didn't want to talk about what might have happened had Alexander survived.

'At any rate, it should be your decision,' Tom rattled on. 'I hardly have the right to make it and there's no one else. I understand it's well enough to travel…I'd be grateful if you could take it today.'

Cass stared at her brother-in-law in confused disbelief. Either he or she had lost the plot somewhere.

'What are you talking about, Tom?'

'The baby.'

'Which baby, Tom?'

A frown questioned whether she'd been listening. 'Pen's baby, of course. It's a girl, this one, did Dray say?'

Cass shook her head to clear it. She must have misunderstood. He couldn't be asking her to take the baby away!

'T-Tom,' she began shakily, 'I'm still not sure…You can't want me to—'

'Yes, I do,' he cut in. 'I've thought about it. In fact, I've thought about little else for days. I know it didn't do anything. It's just a baby. But I can't bring it up.'

Cass ignored her natural inclination to correct his 'it' for a 'she'; Tom was clearly too unbalanced to be accountable.

The question was: how long would his condition last? Days? Weeks? Months? And, meanwhile, who would care for the infant?

Close family? There was just Dray and her. Dray wouldn't be volunteering, and she couldn't. She had nothing to offer a child.

'Listen, Tom,' she spoke in cool, professional tones, 'you are in no state to make such a decision. You've lost your wife. That's devastating enough. And on top of that, you've discovered something fairly distressing about her past. Perhaps you have yet to bond with your baby daughter, but that's-'

'It's not mine!' was torn from Tom and colour suffused his face.

Cass was halted in her tracks. Quite unexpected, but not so far-fetched to induce shock or indignation. She could think of no useful thing to say, so once again said nothing.

It left Tom jumping to the wrong conclusions. 'You knew, didn't you? I told Dray you would.'

Cass shook her head once more; she hadn't even known of the pregnancy.

Tom didn't notice as he stared at the bottom of his glass.

'Is it the same man, the one she was seeing last year,' he added, 'or a new one?'

'I really have no idea, Tom,' she denied. 'I've hardly seen Pen in the last couple of years—'

'No, of course. I forgot.' He gave a laugh that cracked in the middle. 'All those nights away. In town visiting Cass. So easy—with a mobile phone you can pretend to be anywhere. Only she wasn't with you at all.'

He laughed again, a tortured sound. He'd obviously been over this same ground a thousand times in his head but still needed to go over it again.

'Tom, I can't tell you how sorry I am,' she said inadequately and it drew a hard look, more reminiscent of his older brother.

'Are you?' He didn't give her a chance to answer. 'And were you also sorry when you lied for her the time I called?'

Cass had the grace to look ashamed. Without her knowledge, Pen has used her as an alibi, then begged her to back up her story. Cass had been furious and hadn't wanted to do it, but Pen had made her feel if she didn't, the marriage would be over.

'Yes, I *was* sorry…very sorry,' she returned quietly, 'but I thought I was doing the right thing. Pen realised she'd been an idiot and it was you she loved, and she promised never to have another affair.'

'She told me the same,' sneered Tom, 'but only after I made her confess all… You're not a very good liar, Cass, do you know that?'

Cass nodded. Pen had said as much, when Cass had failed to convince Tom that Pen had been with her.

'Your sister was far better,' he added bitterly. 'I actually believed she'd be faithful after that. More fool me.'

'I'm sure she meant to be,' Cass put in softly, wanting to comfort.

But Tom didn't want to be comforted. He wanted the stark truth. 'So what was his name? I have the right to that at least.'

'I don't know, honestly.' Cass could claim that with a clear conscience.

Pen had told her the other man was an executive of Carlisle Electronics but that was all. It didn't seem a wise piece of information to offer now.

Tom looked disbelieving, before saying, 'Well, it doesn't matter. I don't imagine he'll want the baby, anyway.'

'Tom,' she appealed softly, 'why are you sure she isn't yours? Have you had tests done?'

He shook his head. 'I don't need tests to tell me what I already know. The way she was acting…shutting me out…it all falls in place…she must have said something to you!' he insisted.

'Only that you were completely reconciled and planning a family,' she revealed, 'and that was ages ago.'

'When exactly?' he demanded, as if it were important.

'I can't remember a date.' Cass had been doing her first stint in Casualty, with one long week rolling into another. 'Early October, I think.'

His mouth twisted. 'She was lying.'

'I don't think so.' Cass remembered the gist of the conversation and there had been no reason for Pen to lie.

Pen had come to her for medical advice. Tom had been pressing her to start a family and she'd wanted to know the odds on a safe pregnancy.

Cass hadn't minced her words. There had been no way Pen should have had a baby. The risks had been too great. Even with hospitalisation, there had been a forty-per-cent chance of mortality for either her or the baby or both. The only thing she should have done was come clean with Tom about her medical history.

Pen had been horrified at that idea but Cass had pointed out that, if she had embarked on another pregnancy, the doctors would have known it wasn't her first and it was unlikely she'd have kept that from Tom.

Cass had actually believed she'd got through to her. Now she felt she had failed Pen by not pursuing the matter the next time she'd called instead of accepting Pen's assurance that she and Tom had gone off the idea of babies altogether.

'She was lying,' Tom repeated, breaking into her thoughts. 'She was already pregnant, then.'

'What?' Cass was confused.

'In October,' he stressed, 'she was two months gone.'

Cass continued to frown. How could that be? She did some mental arithmetic.

'I thought the baby was premature.' She was sure Dray had told her that.

'We thought so, too, at first,' Tom admitted, 'but the doctors have since said it's full term. They can tell these things.'

Oh, God, Pen, Cass groaned inwardly as she realised what Pen had done. Already pregnant, she'd come to her for approval. When she hadn't given it, she'd decided to bury her head in the sand.

'The dates prove it,' Tom added leadenly.

'Prove what?'

'It isn't mine.'

Cass assumed from this that he had been absent at the time of conception.

'I really am sorry, Tom,' she said gently, but he made a dismissive gesture, as if he didn't want to hear it.

He rose to his feet and she followed, searching for a means to console him.

But it seemed she already had, as he announced, 'Thanks for coming. I feel better now… You won't tell Dray, will you?'

'About the baby?'

'Yes.'

'But if you don't intend keeping her—'

'No, the other baby.' They'd been talking at cross purposes again. 'I don't want him to know. I don't want anybody to know.'

He was adamant and Cass didn't argue. The present was bad enough without dragging in her sister's past.

'Listen, if there's anything else I can do—' she offered without really considering her words.

'It's enough that you're taking the baby away,' he responded, and began walking towards the door.

'But, Tom—' Cass tried to stop him.

Perhaps he didn't hear—or didn't want to—as he left the room without another word.

She went after him, but stopped short as he reached the front hallway. He had joined Dray and their Uncle Charles at the entrance, saying their farewells to the departing mourners.

She didn't want to tackle him again in public so she retraced her steps to the sitting room. She felt unable to run out now. She sat waiting, knowing Dray Carlisle would track her down.

She assumed he must have been aware of what Tom was going to ask of her. It also seemed likely that such a plan had his approval. She was here to take care of an inconvenience.

Cass struggled to get her head round it. They intended her to drop off at the hospital on her way home and pick up the baby. As if it were that simple. As if Cass had no life to rearrange.

No life to give up, because that was what it meant. Tom wanted her to look after her niece *en route* to adoption but Cass knew she couldn't do it. She'd once held another baby, a tiny scrap of humanity that had literally died in her arms.

She remembered how she'd felt then. If ever she held this one, she would never wish to let her go.

She could walk away, of course. No one could stop her. But the thought of Pen's baby, no longer a Carlisle, no longer wanted, kept her there.

She had the briefest of waits before Dray Carlisle appeared. He stood in the doorway, that look of contempt back on his handsome face.

'I can't believe you did that.'

'Did what?'

'Told Tom you'd take the baby away.'

Cass shook her head. She was tired of being misjudged by this family.

'I didn't,' she responded.

'He says you did,' he countered.

And, of course, it was plain whom he preferred to believe.

'I said nothing,' she repeated. 'Tom heard what he wanted to hear.'

He considered this for a moment, blue eyes hooded, before he gave a negligent shrug.

'Whichever,' he dismissed, 'I assume you have no intention of doing so.'

Cass pulled a face in reply. She didn't know what she was going to do, but she resented being put on the spot like this.

'Did you imagine I would? Was that the plan? Get me here for the funeral, then hand her over. Problem solved.'

'Hardly.' He laughed, a harsh sound. 'You're not exactly the maternal type, are you?'

'What do *you* know? You don't know *me*!' she threw back.

His lips thinned. 'Other than in the biblical sense, you mean?'

A dull flush hit Cass's cheeks but she reacted with anger rather than embarrassment.

'That's history,' she seethed. 'Do we have to keep raking it up?'

'Funny, it seemed more current down at the river.' He arched a brow, mocking her. 'Still, you're right. Let's not confuse the issue. Some decisions have to be made concerning your sister's baby. As you'll have gathered, Tom is convinced it's not his—'

'*It* is a *she*,' Cass put in. 'At least call her that.'

His eyes widened a little at the interruption. 'All right, *she*, although the baby's gender is scarcely relevant. Tom's rejection hinges solely on his belief that it...sorry, *she*...was fathered by someone else. The problem is where we proceed from here.'

Was he asking her opinion? He appeared to be. But Cass hadn't had time to form one.

'Tom seems to want her adopted.'

'Yes, and that's probably the best option *if* she isn't his.'

'*If*,' Cass echoed. 'You don't share his conviction?'

'Not totally,' he admitted to her surprise, 'which is why I'd prefer to wait for the result of blood tests.'

She frowned in recollection. 'Tom said he hadn't had any blood tests done.'

He hesitated, before confiding, 'No, but I did. My DNA should be close enough to Tom's to prove or disprove a genetic connection.'

Cass did not dispute it, quizzing instead, 'Tom agreed to this?'

'He signed the necessary documentation, yes,' Dray responded.

A straight enough answer but something in his expression made her wonder.

'He just didn't read it first, perhaps?' she suggested.

A brief smile flickered, acknowledging her astuteness, before he ran on, 'Does it matter? The important thing is to establish paternity.'

'Your test won't do that,' she pointed out, 'unless she *is* Tom's.'

'True,' he conceded. 'Tom says you have no idea of the other candidate.'

'No,' she stated flatly, while her eyes dared him to challenge it.

But he didn't—a fact she would remember later.

'Well, I'll take it from here.' He gripped the door handle, ready to open it.

It took Cass a moment to realise she was being dismissed. 'I can go?'

'Yes.'

Just like that? He really did think she was devoid of feelings.

'Look, if the baby turns out not to be Tom's—'

'Don't worry, I won't call on you.'

Cass should have been relieved. Caring for a baby would seriously disrupt the career which she'd worked so hard to re-establish. But it still hurt that he saw her incapable of doing it.

'Why did you insist I come back to the house?'

'Tom wanted to talk to you. I didn't realise exactly why, otherwise I would have thought twice about it... Still, he seems calmer.'

'Only because he thinks I'll take the baby.'

'Yes, well...if we can leave him thinking it, until alternative arrangements can be made?' He raised a brow, turning it into a request.

She nodded. She had no wish to upset Tom further.

'Thanks,' he murmured briefly. 'We'll go out a side door.'

She followed willingly as he walked her round the far side of the house. They emerged by the garage block where his car stood.

'Richard will take you where you want to go,' he said of the driver who was seated, waiting and ready, in the car.

'Fine.' She wasn't about to argue.

In fact, she would have walked away but he added, 'I imagine this is goodbye.'

'I imagine so,' Cass echoed, keeping her feelings in rigid check.

'Probably wise, considering the effect we have on each other.' His tone was level, as if he were merely stating a fact.

Cass wanted to deny it, to say, You have no effect on me, but her memory wasn't that short, and he was looking at her in a way which recalled all too vividly their encounter in the garden.

It made little sense. To dislike someone this much and still feel such a powerful attraction.

'I have to go.'

Have to run, more like.

He didn't stop her. He wanted her gone, too.

CHAPTER SIX

THERE were good days and bad days. Today was decidedly in the bad category. Assigned to a surgical ward, Cass had been on call from the previous evening and had been paged three times between midnight and seven, before she started her day shift.

Working on so little sleep, she found everything took that much longer because she felt the need to double-check every dosage she wrote on a chart. She was hardly up to speed, when the surgeon, Mr Hunter-Davies, descended to do his round. Always critical, he seemed to take pleasure in asking her opinion on various patients, then ridiculing it.

She was beyond tired by the end of her shift and in need of light relief when she met Chris Wyatt, one of the young male doctors, in the exit lobby.

'The lovely Dr Barker,' he greeted, tongue-in-cheek, as he followed her outside, 'all set for a weekend of high living?'

'How did you guess?'

'Well, if you need company, I may be available.'

'Really?' She arched a brow. 'No new nurses to seduce, Dr Wyatt?'

The suggestion drew a mock offended look, before he disclaimed, 'You shouldn't always believe hospital gossip, Dr Barker. Perhaps I just haven't met the right woman yet.' He let his eyes rest on her, as if she might be the one.

Cass laughed aloud. 'Does this chat-up line usually work for you?'

He grinned incorrigibly. 'You'd be surprised... However, if you require something more original—'

'Thanks, but no, thanks.' Cass had had enough of male

doctors and their egos for today, and began to walk towards the hospital gates.

He fell in step beside her. 'I'll walk you to the tube station.'

'Aren't you on duty?' She looked at the white coat he was wearing.

'Meal break,' he explained, taking it off and slinging it over his shoulder. 'I could do with some fresh air.'

'All right.' Cass didn't argue.

They nodded towards the porter at the entrance, before walking uphill towards the main road. They'd gone about thirty yards when a figure appeared in their path.

Cass stopped dead and fought a desire to turn tail and run.

It had been more than a month since Pen had died and there had been no further word from the Carlisles. Now here was Dray Carlisle, unannounced.

'I need to talk to you,' he stated without preamble.

His voice was taut and there was no mistaking the anger in his eyes. What had she done now?

'Well, I don't need to talk to you.' She moved to step past him.

He blocked her way. 'Five minutes, that's all it will take. Is that unreasonable? I've already waited two hours.'

She pulled a face, saying that wasn't her problem.

'Look, if she doesn't want to talk to you—' began Chris Wyatt, only to be silenced by a glare from Drayton Carlisle.

The young doctor mouthed the word, 'Patient?' at Cass.

She shook her head.

'No, *im*patient,' Dray Carlisle interjected, 'so, do everyone a favour, and disappear.'

'Hey, cool it!' Chris raised his hands and backed off slightly. 'I'm a lover not a fighter...Cass?'

He waited his cue from her.

Cass frowned, wishing he'd used a different expression.

Dray Carlisle's scowl blackened, suggesting imminent loss of temper.

'I'll be fine,' she said with more confidence than she felt.

'Okay.' Chris gave her no argument but turned back towards the hospital.

'So is he?' Dray demanded the moment they were alone.

'Is he?' she echoed. 'Is he what?'

'One of your lovers?' Contempt laced his words.

'Don't be ridiculous,' she dismissed. 'He's a colleague. Nothing more.'

'A fellow doctor?'

'Yes.'

She caught up with what he'd said. He now knew she was a doctor?

His mouth twisted slightly before he switched to asking, 'Is there a pub around here?'

'At the top of the road. Why?'

'We could go for a drink.'

'What?'

Did he really think she'd want to go anywhere with him after the way he'd just talked to her?

'Or alternatively,' he went on, 'we could stand here and wash our dirty linen in public. It's up to you.'

He glanced down the road to the hospital. A group of nurses was gathered at the gates. Cass recognised a couple from her ward.

'Yes, all right.' She didn't want to be the focus of hospital gossip.

She started up the hill, leaving him to fall in step beside her. They passed his car where he must have been sitting, watching for her, and walked to the top of the road in silence. She thought of losing him before they reached the pub but there wasn't much chance of it.

Though the Star and Garter was the nearest pub to the hospital, Cass had never actually been inside. It was cool, dimly lit and the background music not too intrusive. At six in the evening it was also half empty. She saw a couple of student doctors at a table near the door and opted to sit at a more private booth in the rear while Dray Carlisle went to order drinks.

He came back with what looked like lager in a tall glass and the dry white wine she'd requested.

She waited for him to break the silence but he seemed in no hurry. She glanced up and caught him staring. He continued to do so until she looked away again.

'So why are you here?' She forced the issue.

'I need to speak to you,' he repeated what he'd said earlier, 'and, as you haven't returned any of my calls, you gave me little choice.'

'Calls? What calls?'

'I've left at least three messages on your answering service in the last forty-eight hours.'

'I've been on duty.'

He looked sceptical. 'I also phoned the hospital and was informed there was no auxiliary called Cassandra Barker, only a junior doctor, and the said doctor could be paged if I knew her number but not otherwise…I assume that is you.'

She nodded and couldn't resist a dry, 'Amazing, isn't it, what us lower orders can achieve, given half a chance?'

'Isn't it just?' he drawled back. 'I would say congratulations, but you'd no doubt interpret it as patronising. What I find even more amazing is the fact that your sister never mentioned your new profession.'

Cass shrugged. Pen wouldn't have wanted Cass upstaging her in any respect.

'I don't imagine you ever showed much interest, did you?' She tried to make it his negligence, not Pen's.

But he took her aback by saying, 'As a matter of fact, I did ask about you from time to time. She'd say you were working in some hamburger place or allude to whichever man you were currently dating, but I don't remember any reference to medical school. When did you graduate?'

'A year ago.'

'Then you must have been at university at the time we first met.'

'No, I was a checkout girl then, remember?' She deliberately brought up her past so he'd know she wasn't ashamed of it.

His brow creased and Cass guessed that he was now wondering whether she really was a bona fide doctor, and not some lunatic posing as one.

'I went straight from school to university to study medicine,' she explained, 'but took a couple of years out, midway through, before returning to qualify.'

She wasn't going to admit that he'd acted as her incentive in some convoluted way.

'Why did you leave in the first place?' He still sounded suspicious.

'Circumstances.'

'Which were?'

That, she couldn't tell him and keep her promise to Tom concerning Pen's first pregnancy.

'What is this—the Spanish Inquisition?'

His mouth thinned. 'I'm just trying to square your past with your present. I don't recall your even hinting at any of this during our brief relationship.'

She hadn't. A sense of failure had left her reluctant to discuss her apparently aborted medical course.

'Unsettle you, does it,' she said now, 'shop assistants getting above their station?'

He shook his head. It was a gesture of exasperation rather than denial.

'Still fighting the class war, Cass? And long after the rest of us have given up and gone home. Don't you ever get bored with it?'

He clearly was, as his voice slowed to a languid drawl.

Cass, who had been spoiling for a fight, was disarmed.

'Well, I'm certainly bored with this meeting, so if we could get to the point—'

'Fine.'

He reached into his jacket pocket, drew out a white envelope and laid it in front of her.

Cass's name and address was scrawled on the front, but no stamp or postmark. It took her a moment to recognise the handwriting. She made no move to pick it up.

'This was found among your sister's things,' he continued at length. 'It didn't seem appropriate to post it.'

Cass nodded. It was a big enough shock like this. 'Have you read what's in it?'

His mouth tightened with annoyance. 'I do have some scruples.'

'Has Tom?' she added.

He shook his head. 'Tom asked my housekeeper, Mrs Henderson, to clear out your sister's drawers and wardrobes. She brought the letter to me, worried it might upset Tom further.'

'How is Tom?' Her concern was genuine.

He hesitated before admitting, 'Somewhat irrational.'

Cass's eyes narrowed, wondering what irrational covered, but he didn't expand on it. Instead he added, 'Do you want to know about the baby?'

Her heart and her head went their separate ways on this, one screaming yes, the other no. Her face remained expressionless.

He assumed indifference and continued abruptly, 'Well, I'll tell you, anyway. The DNA testing proved a genetic link between Tom and the baby.'

'So he accepts he's the father,' Cass surmised with relief.

'Not quite.' He didn't look at her this time, but nursed his glass as he relayed, 'Tom accepts the baby was fathered by a Carlisle, just not by him.'

'But who else could—?' Cass broke off, and her eyes fixed on the man opposite her.

'I see you've reached the same conclusion as my brother.' His drawl suggested it didn't bother him.

Because it wasn't true? Or because it was?

He returned her questioning gaze with a mocking look.

No, it couldn't be true. Whatever she thought of Dray Carlisle, he wouldn't have done that to his brother.

'Why don't you open the letter? Who knows, all may be revealed.'

It was a challenge. She wondered if he knew, without reading it, what was in this letter. Had her sister confided in him?

She finally picked it up and turned it round. She froze for a moment when she saw the back of the envelope. Where the V had been pasted down, her sister had stuck a label and written across in neat, printed letters, 'TO BE SENT SHOULD ANYTHING HAPPEN TO ME'. She had done it in such a way that the letter couldn't be opened, read and resealed.

Cass inserted a fingernail under a corner flap and ripped the top across. She took out the pages inside and unfolded them with a feeling of dread, made worse by Dray Carlisle's presence.

She read a couple of lines. 'Dear Cass, If you're reading this, then I guess things haven't worked out too well for me,' and then crumpled the letter in her hand.

'Excuse me.' She stood up and he rose with her, perhaps meaning to block her way again. 'I have to go to the loo.'

He looked suspicious but he glanced at her bag, still sitting in the corner of the booth, and didn't try to stop her.

She didn't really need the loo, of course. It was privacy she was seeking as she locked herself in one of two cubicles in the dingy pub toilet.

She read the letter slowly, tears threatening. It sounded so like Pen. Though it was patently a 'in the event of my demise' letter, it was surprisingly upbeat, as if by writing it Pen had thought somehow it would ward off death.

In it Pen explained that she had, indeed, been pregnant when she'd sought out advice from Cass and, despite Cass's negative reaction, had wanted to go through with it, especially once Tom had found out. 'He was over the moon about the baby.' She'd considered telling him the whole truth but it would have spoiled things. He'd taken ages to forgive and forget last year's indiscretion. 'So why hurt him more by dredging up the past?'

She was attending a hospital in London for her antenatal care and, with any luck, could keep Tom in the dark about dates and other specifics—at least until the baby was born. After that, she was confident he'd forgive her anything.

Should everything 'go pear-shaped,' however, she hoped Cass would step in to sort things out and ensure the baby was well looked after.

Pen didn't say how. Or precisely what *things* would need sorting. She just accepted Cass would somehow make it all right.

Perhaps she believed her final message—'Tell Tom I really did love him'—would be like waving a magic wand.

Perhaps she thought by signing it, 'Always, your loving little sister' the past would tug at Cass's heartstrings and stop her feeling used.

Cass read the letter a second time and the threat of tears receded. Three years and she'd hardly seen Pen, and yet, here she was, expecting her to clear up the mess she'd left behind. The presumption angered Cass and that was before she noticed the postscript scribbled on the back of the letter.

'P.S. Sorry about the Dray business but he really wasn't right for you. Too mean and moody by half, and I should know. Still sexy, though, so watch out!!!'

It reopened old wounds and left Cass wondering for what exactly was Pen apologising. The phrasing also jarred.

'Too mean and moody by half, and I should know.'

Why should Pen know? And was that 'still sexy' merely banter or a remark based on firsthand experience?

Cass shook her head. No, Tom's crazy idea couldn't be true. She didn't want to believe it, and yet—

'Hello?' a voice from the other side of the cubicle interrupted her thoughts. 'Dr Barker, is that you?'

Cass didn't recognise the speaker and called back, 'Yes, who's that?'

'Student Nurse Clemens,' came the nervous reply. 'Sorry to bother you, but your…um…friend asked me to check you were okay.'

Cass muttered a silent curse, and, flushing the toilet for show, emerged to find a young girl, hovering anxiously. She was vaguely familiar.

Cass said, 'I'm fine,' and they traded fixed smiles before the embarrassed girl scuttled into the cubicle.

Washing her hands, Cass counted slowly to ten before leaving the toilet.

She was still furious, however, as she approached the booth.

'All right?' he enquired, rising slightly.

'How dare you do that?' she snapped at him, and stretched for her shoulder bag.

He guessed her intention and, with frighteningly fast reactions, took it from her, preventing her from leaving.

'I was worried,' he replied heavily.

'Like hell,' she grated out between clenched teeth. 'Give me my bag back!'

'Sit down first!' he instructed.

Cass seethed in frustration as he placed the bag on his side, out of her reach. Any other pub in any other part of London, and she might have created a scene until he gave it back. But the bar was filling up with doctors and nurses and students, and she certainly didn't want the notoriety of being witnessed in a violent argument with some man.

She sat but she was literally shaking with anger.

'Look, I'm sorry.' He tried to take the heat out of the situation. 'You'd been gone a long time and I was concerned. I simply asked the girl when she was entering the ladies—'

'The girl is a nurse,' she replied heavily, 'a student nurse over whom I nominally have authority. Checking up on me in the toilet, I'm sure, has made me rise immeasurably in her esteem.'

He raised a mild brow. 'I didn't realise your dignity was of such importance to you.'

Cass glared back. He made her sound pompous and she wasn't. It was just hard enough gaining professional respect as a doctor, if you were young and female.

'Remind me to swan into your boardroom one day,' she retaliated, 'and see how happy you'd be, your personal life intruding into your professional.'

He didn't seem fazed by the idea, murmuring, 'I'd survive.'

As chief executive, he probably would. As chief executive, he could do what he damn well pleased.

'I suppose they've ceased being surprised by *your* personal life,' she muttered back.

His eyes narrowed in the first sign of annoyance. 'Meaning?'

'Work it out.' Cass didn't feel like spelling out the obvious.

'There's nothing particularly untoward about my personal life,' he claimed frankly. 'I date women, and if I like them, I sleep with them, no expectations on either side. I believe that would be regarded as fairly normal in this day and age.'

So smooth, Cass thought, so untroubled by conscience or morals. He had it all taped.

'It's with *whom* you sleep that might be the issue.'

'Yes, well, admittedly my judgement could be faulted on occasion.'

His eyes lingered on Cass, making the remark personal to her.

'I expect it could,' she responded, 'if it included your brother's wife.'

She matched his cool but inside her was a hard, painful knot of anger.

He barely reacted. A flicker of pulse at his temple, a tightening of the jaw line.

'Is that an accusation or a question?'

'Whichever.'

'Well, if it's an accusation, I assume you have some grounds for making it, and, if it's a question, could you make it more specific?'

Cass had been praying for a flat denial, not this double-talk. She felt a little sick inside. She masked it with contempt.

'Were you sleeping with my sister?' She wondered if that was specific enough for him.

The eyes narrowing on her face said it was, although he clearly didn't like the question. No outrage, of course, just that upper-class disdain.

'Does she say so in her missive?' He arched one of those straight dark brows and Cass wanted to pick up the heavy glass ashtray and do him damage.

How had she ever loved this man? How had she once been so blind as to believe him worth loving?

'What do you think?' She meant to leave him guessing.

She meant to leave him full stop as she stretched a hand for her bag, only to have him grab her arm and force her to sit once more.

'*I think,*' he replied heavily, 'that perfectly healthy young women do not write farewell letters before they die in childbirth. Therefore *I think* your sister had reason to believe she was at risk and wrote to her nearest female relative to, some-what optimistically, ask her to care for her baby should Tom discover it wasn't his... Am I warm?'

He had the gist, although Pen hadn't asked her outright to care for the baby—only to make sure it was cared for—and Cass was more interested in what he'd as good as admitted.

'You knew,' she accused, 'didn't you? That the baby wasn't Tom's... That the baby was yours.'

She finally hit a nerve, beating a tattoo at the side of his temple, and, for a moment, the hand gripping hers became painful, before he removed it altogether, as if touching her was suddenly distasteful to him.

'I knew—*know* no such thing,' he grated back, 'and, if you imagine that I'll look after the baby permanently, you and Tom are sadly mistaken. So, unless you have something else to say...'

He raised his glass to drain it.

Cass stared at him in surprise. It was the last solution she'd imagined, him looking after her sister's baby.

Charcoal suit, silk shirt, tie loosened at the collar but every inch the businessman and as masculine as they came. Bright as they came, too. Just not new man material.

He'd obviously said his piece, as he rose to his feet and, handing over her bag, waited for her to follow.

Cass could have stayed, just to make a point, but she felt her presence would have already stirred enough curiosity on the hospital grapevine.

It was still light when they left the pub. She thought he'd walk away but he didn't, saying instead, 'I'll give you a lift.'

'No, thanks.' She'd had enough emotional battering for the day. 'It's quicker by tube.'

'Probably.' He didn't argue.

They exchanged looks, waiting for the other to say good-bye; oddly, now it came down to it, neither seemed in a hurry to get away.

Cass had a question to ask. It had been in her mind since the funeral, and weighed heavier with each day passing. But did she really want to know the answer?

'Listen, about the baby—' she began impulsively, then dried at his surprised look.

'Yes?'

'I—I...where is she now?'

A frown etched on his forehead as he considered his answer. It was hardly encouraging when it came, a simple, 'Why?'

'I'm concerned for her, of course.' Did he think she had no feelings at all?

It seemed so, as his mouth thinned into a sceptical line. 'She's been dealt with.'

Dealt with? It was a horrible expression when applied to a baby.

'In what way?' Cass demanded.

'Don't worry, she's been fed and watered,' he drawled back.

Was that meant to be reassuring? Cass didn't think so. She bit her lip to stop herself asking whether her niece was being held and rocked and loved. He would only mock.

She confined herself to an unemotional, 'Babies need stimulating, even in the first months of life, or their ability to bond is impaired.'

He studied her briefly before replying, 'If I need a textbook on child rearing, *Doctor*, I'll purchase one. However, if you're about to volunteer some practical help...?'

Would he accept it? Somehow Cass doubted it.

'I would if I could,' she said on the defensive, 'but I do have a career, one I'm working very hard to establish.'

She sounded pompous again and half expected him to make capital out of it.

Instead he took it at face value, saying, 'I realise that and I didn't come here to persuade you otherwise.'

'Then why?' Not to play postman, Cass was sure of that.

He took a moment to answer, considering his words first. 'I'd hoped your sister might have given positive confirmation of Tom as the father, but, from your reaction, she obviously hasn't.'

'No,' she agreed, 'that honour's still up for grabs... Pity neither of you wants it.'

It was a throwaway remark but he caught it and the flash of anger on his face told her she'd gone too far. She turned away from him, only to be pulled back by a hand on her arm.

'You're so sure I slept with your sister—why is that?' he challenged harshly.

Cass wasn't *so* sure but the very question fuelled her suspicions. 'You have yet to deny it.'

'Oh, and that makes it conclusive? Or is it knowing what a friendly girl your sister was?'

'Meaning?'

'Well, let's just say had I wanted it—' his mouth twisted '—the offer was there.'

True or not, it struck Cass as a vile thing to say.

'You're such a bastard, Dray Carlisle—' She tried to jerk free.

He wouldn't let her, grabbing her other arm to drag her closer. 'Really. You didn't think so once. Remember?'

He held her roughly, his hands bruising, his chest a rigid wall against hers, yet it made no difference: her body was suddenly alive.

'I remember nothing!' she threw back.

'Liar!' He bared his teeth, half laugh, half growl. 'Let's see, shall we.'

Oblivious of passers-by, he gathered her into his arms and, lowering his head to hers, kissed her hard on the mouth.

Equally oblivious, she pushed at his chest, fingers digging into flesh, body straining, resisting even as her lips parted and her eyes closed, even as a helpless moan came from her throat until she was kissing him back, tasting him as he tasted her, responding to a need so fundamental it defied pride or sense.

When he finally raised his head away, it was to murmur into her hair, '*I remember.* I remember all of it: the touch of you, the sounds you made, the way we were together...'

'*Don't.*' Cass trembled, remembering it too, as he moved his lips from her temple to her cheek, seeking her mouth in another deeply sensual kiss that had her arms sliding round his neck.

She shut her eyes once more and let her mind play tricks. It was three years ago. She loved this man and he loved her. He'd used the actual words. Made it all seem right, this frightening, consuming passion they had for each other.

Now past and present merged and, raising his head, he gazed down at her as if his eyes could reach her very soul. How could he have looked at her like this and not felt something?

She shook her head in denial. 'It was never real.'

'Wasn't it?' A hand lifted to smooth her cheek. 'You and I—it feels real to me, Cassie.'

Cassie? Another echo from the past. Once he had called her that and she'd liked it, but that girl had gone.

Yes, she remembered. The trouble was she remembered it too well. For three weeks she'd lived in a fantasy world, her head in the clouds, her heart tripping over. Then suddenly she'd been brought crashing back to earth. It seemed he'd grown bored and moved on. Perhaps if he'd told her to her face, she could have borne it better. But he'd left Pen to do his dirty work. The pain of it had left her stricken, heartbroken. That was her reality.

With no wish to relive it, she killed any errant desire for him, and, when he made to kiss her again, turned her face away.

'There is no you and I, Dray,' she dismissed in a cold, hard voice. 'There never was. There's just sex and I'm not that desperate at the moment… Still, I'll bear you in mind, if you like.'

The last she added to sound indifferent, as if she could take or leave him.

She heard the sharp intake of his breath as his head jerked back, saw the tenderness go from his eyes, felt the hands suddenly hurting on her waist, but she didn't care. It was only a fraction of the hurt he'd once inflicted on her.

She watched as his expression changed to anger at being thwarted. Too bad. Had he really believed she'd be fooled twice?

'Don't bother,' he finally snarled in response. 'I prefer my women more exclusive than a revolving door.'

'What? Like your brother's wife, for instance?' she sneered back, attacking him rather than her sister, and wrenched free from his arms.

She didn't wait for a reply but marched away, blind with rage, trembling with fury, and didn't look back. She wiped at her mouth until she could taste only bitterness.

She would not forget the past.

CHAPTER SEVEN

A FORTNIGHT later Cass stood on the step of North Dean Hall and composed herself before ringing the bell. It was just possible he was at home, although unlikely, mid-week. He would be at work, making another million.

When no one came, she rang again. Eventually a bolt was drawn back behind the heavy double oak doors, and Mrs Henderson, the housekeeper, appeared.

'Yes?' The woman seemed flustered.

'It's Cassandra Barker, the late Mrs Carlisle's sister,' she said helpfully. 'I telephoned last week.'

'Yes, of course.' Mrs Henderson recalled their brief conversation and finally recognised her. 'I'm afraid Mr Carlisle's not at home. Was he expecting you?'

'Not specifically today. I was in the area and came on the off chance to see my niece.'

She tried to sound casual, though inside she felt anything but. She'd spent a week fretting over how exactly the baby had been 'dealt with', then another worried by the discovery that her niece was currently living at North Dean Hall.

'If that's all right?' Cass smiled disarmingly at the older lady.

Mrs Henderson managed a smile in return but still seemed distracted. 'I imagine so...I can't think Mr Carlisle would mind.'

Fortunately she was talking to herself.

Cass, of course, knew Drayton *would* very much mind. It didn't stop her stepping inside.

'If you come through to the drawing room—' Mrs

Henderson led the way '—I'll bring some refreshments, then fetch the baby... She's asleep at the moment.'

'Don't waken her on my account,' Cass replied as they entered the room. 'I can wait.'

'Well, if you're sure...' Mrs Henderson looked relieved. 'Would you like tea or coffee?'

'Coffee.'

The housekeeper nodded, then left Cass alone.

Cass could have sat down but she preferred to stand. In fact, she paced restlessly around the room.

She'd got past the first hurdle but still felt tense. She was here on false pretences. Had Dray imagined she would call like this, he would have warned Mrs Henderson to bar her from the house.

Nor was Cass certain she was doing the right thing. Her hospital contract had come to an end and just yesterday she'd heard from a practice in Slough, willing to train her as a family doctor. Her career was progressing as planned. She could move out of London and start a new life. She didn't have to take along any unnecessary baggage.

The trouble was the very words—*unnecessary baggage*— had her feeling sick at heart. Applied to a baby, they ranked alongside Dray Carlisle's 'dealt with' and made her no better than he was.

Perhaps she was worse. What did a businessman like Dray know of the needs of an infant? But *she* knew. She understood that a child shouldn't be passed round like a parcel because the address on it wasn't too clear. Yet, so far, she had done nothing about it, apart from one call last week and it had simply confirmed the child's whereabouts.

Even now she'd come with reluctance, driven by a guilty conscience and a need for reassurance. After Pen's death, she'd allowed Dray Carlisle to shut her out. But since Pen's letter, she hadn't been able to stop thinking of her little niece. She still had no idea what Pen would have wanted her to do, but she had to do something. Perhaps if she saw the baby was well cared for, that would be it and she could let it go.

Cass waited ten, then fifteen minutes, before deciding she could stand waiting no longer. She walked along the corridor to the kitchens at the side of the house, guided by the sound of crying.

A pram stood in one corner, empty. The wailing came from Mrs Henderson's arms, a small red-faced bundle screaming the house down. On a surface lay a puddle of milk and an overturned baby's bottle. Along from it was a kettle, almost ready to boil.

A visibly distressed Mrs Henderson relayed, 'I was rushing too much. It slipped out of my hand. I'm sorry about your coffee but she woke—'

'It's all right.' Cass had already taken in the situation and just wanted to be helpful. 'I'll hold her if you want, while you make up another bottle.'

She crossed to take the baby, surrendered willingly by the older woman. The infant continued to cry, but Cass remained calm, curving her into her shoulder, as she murmured soothing noises and began to walk up and down the kitchen until the new bottle was ready. It took a while as the milk had to be cooled but the baby's crying subsided to a less distressed level and she took her bottle eagerly when it arrived.

Cass sat on a Windsor chair to feed her new niece. Up till that point, she had been indistinguishable from any of the other crying babies Cass had encountered in her short spell in Paediatrics. Now Cass could see her rosebud mouth, blue eyes, a cap of dark hair and long sweep of lashes. She bore little resemblance to her sister Pen, but Cass still felt a rush of immediate love, frightening in its strength. She knew then why she had kept away.

'I can't thank you enough,' Mrs Henderson ran on warmly. 'Normally I have her feed ready but she woke sooner than I expected and I'm afraid I get terribly flustered when she's crying.'

'It's hard, I know,' Cass replied in sympathetic tones. 'You get very torn. Have you thought of preparing a few feeds in advance?'

'Can you do that?' Mrs Henderson said in surprise.

Cass nodded, adding the proviso, 'The teats must remain sterilised and the bottles should be stored somewhere separate in your fridge.'

'That would certainly make life easier.' A sigh escaped the housekeeper's lips. 'I mean I do enjoy taking care of her, but having never had one of my own...'

'You can't be expected to know.' Cass's eyes rested momentarily on the housekeeper.

She was a trim, upright woman who looked reasonably fit, but she was closer to sixty than fifty. Did Dray Carlisle really imagine the woman could cope with the house *and* a baby?

'I suppose I should have asked that girl,' Mrs Henderson added.

'Girl?' Cass echoed.

'Melanie.' Disapproval clouded the older woman's eyes. 'The temporary nanny.'

'Is it her day off?' Cass enquired.

Mrs Henderson shook her head. 'She walked out yesterday. No warning. Just up and decided she'd had enough...I haven't told Mr Carlisle yet.'

Hadn't he noticed? Cass was appalled. How could he *not* notice?

'He's in America,' her unspoken question was answered. 'Mrs Carlisle—Mr Simon's wife—felt it best to wait his return. I only hope he doesn't hold me responsible.'

'Why should he do that?' Cass tried to sound reassuring, despite firsthand experience of Dray's autocratic ways.

Mrs Henderson was hesitant. 'I don't want to talk out of turn...'

'That's all right.' Cass didn't press her.

But it was obviously preying on the housekeeper's mind. 'It's just that the girl was happy enough before Mr Carlisle left,' she confided, 'only I don't think Ellie was the main attraction.'

Cass guessed who was, but she didn't comment. It was too close to home, Dray Carlisle and his easy conquests.

Instead her eyes returned to the baby, a small perfect being, no longer nameless but Ellie. Whose choice? she wondered.

'Do you wish me to take her?' Mrs Henderson finally thought to ask. 'Or will I make that coffee I promised?'

'Coffee, please. I'll have it here, if that's all right.'

'Are you sure? I can easily bring it through to the drawing room—'

Cass shook her head. 'To be honest, I'm not used to being waited on and I'll be more comfortable in the kitchen.'

The housekeeper was disarmed by her frankness, but gradually relaxed as they sat together at the table, drinking coffee.

'You're very good with her.' Mrs Henderson watched Cass amuse the baby after she'd lost interest in her bottle.

'I did a lot of babysitting for neighbours when I was younger,' Cass explained.

'I wish I had more experience,' Mrs Henderson sighed. 'Myself and Bob were never blessed.'

'You'll manage.' Cass wanted to convince herself as well as the housekeeper.

She was just deciding it was time to make leaving noises when the telephone rang. She could only hear one side of the conversation, but it was enough to realise that something had happened to Mrs Henderson's husband.

When the caller rang off, the housekeeper relayed that her husband had broken his hip while cutting the hedge round their cottage and had been admitted to the hospital.

'I'll have to go,' she said first, then shook her head, 'but, of course, I can't. Who'd look after the baby?'

She was talking to herself rather than Cass, and Cass resisted the impulse to offer her help. She'd promised herself that she would not get involved.

'How about Camilla, Simon's wife?' she suggested.

'I never thought…' Mrs Henderson considered the possibility. 'She might, yes.'

The housekeeper telephoned and was visibly relieved on receiving an answer, but it quickly became apparent that Camilla Carlisle wasn't eager to help out.

'Mrs Camilla has guests,' she explained afterwards, 'but she's promised to come later and collect Ellie for the night. I'll just have to hang on.'

Cass could have left it. A broken hip was rarely life threatening. But the worry on Mrs Henderson's face combined with Ellie's vulnerability made her say, 'No, you go. I'll look after the baby till she shows.'

'I couldn't ask that of you!' the housekeeper protested.

'You're not asking,' Cass pointed out. 'I'm offering.'

'But still. I don't know—'

'Look, it's no hardship. I love babies and Ellie is my niece.'

'Well, yes, of course.' Mrs Henderson didn't doubt Cass's right to care for the baby and, rather than argue with her, accepted gratefully, 'If you're absolutely sure—'

'Totally,' Cass lied—this wasn't the brief visit she'd planned.

But Mrs Henderson took her at her word and, after a flurry of activity, was out of the door and into her car, speeding off to see her husband.

Well, it was only a couple of hours, Cass reasoned. Not long enough to get attached.

Certainly Ellie didn't seem to mind a new face as Cass laid her on a plastic mat on the table and changed her nappy, tickling toes and kissing feet, drawing smiles and gurgles of baby laughter. With enough stimulation and affection, she'd probably be an easy baby to look after.

The question was: how would she be without them?

Cass shook her head. She wasn't going to make it her problem. She would enjoy this time with her niece and store it away with all the other family memories.

It was a beautiful day so Cass decided on a walk. She placed the baby in the big coach pram and took a key from the board to lock the back door behind her.

She went round the side of the house to the front, then slowly down the driveway. Overhanging tree branches formed a canopy through which the summer sun filtered and the baby stared upwards, fascinated by the dance of shadow and light on her face. Cass felt a similar sense of wonder in staring at her.

All babies were beautiful, but some more so than others. Ellie was one of the 'more-so's, with large eyes set in an oval-shaped face and the promise of abundant dark hair to come.

It only made the situation more poignant. Most couples would be delighted to have such a baby, yet here she was motherless, and, to all intents and purposes, fatherless unless one of the Carlisles decided otherwise. Looking at her now, Cass wondered how either could resist claiming her as their own.

In another life, Cass could have done so readily, but not in this one. For what had she to offer? No real home and no money apart from what she earned.

Cass doubted Ellie would thank her if she were like Pen in nature. A lack of money had blighted Pen's childhood, but how much worse would it have been if there had been an alternative, a life of luxury denied her?

Because that was what the Carlisles seemed to be offering. No emotional commitment, perhaps, but still a place in the family as one of them. Why else had Dray Carlisle brought her home when he could so easily have allowed her to be put up for adoption?

And what could Cass offer? Love, that was all. Once she would have believed it enough. Once she'd loved Pen and thought she could make everything right for her. But Pen had never been happy, had always looked for something else even when she'd appeared to have everything: money, the big house, a husband who loved her. So what had been missing?

Cass wasn't sure but it made her question if she'd be any more successful with Pen's daughter.

'Ellie,' she said aloud and smiled at the baby gazing up at her.

She really was lovely, as was her name. Cass wondered who had chosen it: Tom or Dray or even Pen before she'd died?

It seemed unlikely to be Tom who'd referred to her as simply 'it' when Cass had seen him after the funeral, and it didn't sound like something Pen would have favoured, but if it were Dray, then didn't that indicate his possible paternity?

Indicate? Who was she kidding? His taking the baby into his home positively *broadcast* the fact.

She just had to accept it. Dray Carlisle had slept with her sister. Why should it be a big deal to her? Her feelings for him had surely died many years ago. It was Tom they'd really betrayed. It was Tom who must be devastated at this double act of treachery.

In her case it was surely a case of hurt pride, reminding her of what a fool she'd been all those years ago. God, how easy she'd been!

No wonder he believed she slept around. She'd never felt that way for anyone. Pure lust, though she'd called it love at the time. Not to him, of course. Even, at the height of her madness, she hadn't trusted him enough to use the word love.

But he had used it and that was the real crime in Cass's

eyes. He hadn't needed to: she'd already been sleeping with him, already been crazy about him. To say 'I love you' was gratuitous unless it was meant, so she'd assumed he'd meant it. How naive could you get?

She wondered now had he said it to Pen. Maybe he had and meant it in her case, making baby Ellie truly a love child. Was that better or worse? For Ellie, better, she supposed, but it left the sour taste of jealousy in her mouth.

Cass swallowed hard to rid herself of it and continued down the winding driveway. She stopped short of the lodge house, fearing Uncle Charles might see her. He'd always been pleasant to her in the past but who knew what Dray had said about her since the funeral?

She strolled back up to the main house and let herself in through the back door. Ellie was once more asleep and she used the breathing space to make up a couple of feeds, then waited for Camilla Carlisle to show.

She'd promised to appear at five o'clock but it was nearer six when she turned up. From the outset, the woman made it plain she was doing so on sufferance.

'Oh, I was expecting Mrs Henderson. Who are you?' She stood on the doorstep, looking Cass over in a supercilious manner.

Cass wasn't surprised at her lack of recognition. They'd met only briefly at the wedding and she wasn't the type to be particularly interested in other women.

'Cass Barker,' she introduced herself, 'Pen's sister.'

The woman's expression changed to dislike in an instant. 'What are *you* doing here?'

'I came to visit my niece,' Cass stated the obvious.

Camilla Carlisle continued to scowl. 'Does Dray know you're here?'

'No.' Cass wasn't going to lie. 'I came on spec, but, don't worry, I'm not contemplating kidnap or anything.'

'Pity,' the woman clipped back. 'It might solve all our

problems, but then I understand you're too busy with your career.'

She made it sound as though Cass were ducking her responsibilities.

Cass dropped any attempt at politeness, saying, 'Some of us have a living to earn. We haven't married money.'

'Like your sister, you mean?' A lip curled in contempt. 'You certainly can't be referring to me. I have my own trust fund.'

'How nice for you.' Cass's flat tone said she was unimpressed. 'That must have made you popular.'

'Implying what?' This time Camilla Carlisle's face mottled with anger.

Cass realised she'd touched a nerve but decided not to pursue it. The conversation had already descended too far.

'Forget it,' she dismissed and switched to relaying, 'Mrs Henderson has already gone to the hospital and Ellie's taking a nap at the moment. I've made up some bottles for her. You'll find them in the fridge.'

She stood aside to let Camilla Carlisle enter.

The woman remained on the doorstep. 'Well, it sounds as if you have everything under control, so I'll leave you to it.'

'What?' Cass stared at her in disbelief.

'I'll leave you to it,' Camilla Carlisle repeated with evident satisfaction and turned on her heel to walk back towards her silver saloon.

Cass followed rapidly, saying, 'Hold on! Mrs Henderson said you'd take Ellie tonight.'

'Only as an absolute necessity,' the older woman responded, unlocking her door and climbing in, 'and now you're here, it isn't.'

'I can't stay!' Cass hung onto the door rim before it could be shut. 'And, even if I could, Dray Carlisle would violently object to my remaining in his house.'

'Would he?' Speculative eyes trained on her. 'Now why would that be?'

Cass wasn't about to tell this woman anything. 'He won't want a virtual stranger in his home, that's all.'

'In case you steal the family silver?' Camilla Carlisle suggested nastily. 'No matter, he's insured… Now, if you could shut my door—' A superior brow was arched in her direction.

'Shut it yourself.' Cass turned to walk away.

The mutter of 'How common!' was pitched loud enough for Cass to hear, but Camilla Carlisle didn't wait around for a response.

Gravel was thrown up as she reversed her car in the court-yard, then accelerated down the drive.

Cass had to be content with making faces at the retreating vehicle. Pen had always said Camilla Carlisle was a cow but until now Cass had kept an open mind.

She went back into the house, wondering what she should do. Call Mrs Henderson and ask her to return? Not knowing which hospital she'd gone to made that difficult. Or take Ellie back to London with her? No, for all sorts of reasons, she couldn't do that. So what options were left?

None apart from staying.

When Ellie woke again, she fed her from one of the pre-pared bottles, then went on a tour of the first and second floors until she found a makeshift nursery at the top of the house. She placed Ellie in a carrycot while she looked round. The wallpaper of sailboats and ships clearly dated from an earlier age but there was no shortage of cot toys that rattled and squeaked and a mirrored light that also played music and a beautiful mobile that danced around at the touch of a switch. A changing table stood in one corner with a neatly stacked supply of nappies and wipes, while a chest of drawers contained the prettiest, most exclusive of baby-wear. They were, of course, only material things and didn't constitute proof of any real concern for Ellie.

She selected a towelling sleep suit and carried Ellie to the bathroom along the corridor. There she found a yellow plastic baby bath and, setting it on its stand, filled it with tepid water. At two months Ellie was too young for bath toys but she smiled and kicked as Cass splashed her playfully and rocked her gently in the water.

She had no idea of Ellie's routine but she went downstairs again and gave her a last feed in the kitchen, sitting next to the still warm Aga.

It was not yet nine but Cass decided to have an early night, too, and switched off lights as she went back upstairs.

On the first floor she briefly trespassed in Dray's bedroom to borrow a shirt and toothbrush, before continuing up to the nursery floor. She put Ellie on her back in the cot, switched on the mirrored light and off the overhead one. The baby cried a little in protest, but, rather than lift her out again, Cass stayed with her, singing and crooning, until gradually her eyelids drooped and she gave up the battle to stay awake.

Cass slipped away to take a quick shower in the bathroom, re-dressing in the borrowed shirt. She smoothed out her trousers and top for the morning and washed her smalls in the sink, draping them over a heated towel rail to dry. Then, checking on Ellie for a final time and clicking off the mirrored light in the cot, she went to bed in the adjoining room.

Despite being in a strange house and even stranger situation, Cass wasn't awake for long. It was part of her training— to grab sleep when and where she could, and sleep through everything but the sound of her bleeper. Other sounds might register but they usually became part of her dreams unless, of course, they were persistent and too loud to ignore.

A baby's crying, for example. At first it was merely background noise, an adjunct to the scene playing in her head, until it escalated to a pitch too real to be part of the dream state.

That was another skill learned as a busy hospital doctor.

One moment to be fast asleep, the next bolt upright in bed, conscious and reacting. Mere seconds later, she was out of bed and through the adjoining door, reassuring, 'I'm here, Ellie.'

She took a couple of steps towards the crying baby, then stopped dead. The nursery was still in darkness but a sliver of moonlight crept in round the edge of the curtain and she saw a shadowy figure looming over the cot.

For a split second she imagined it was a genuine intruder and fear gripped her.

A voice breathed, 'Melanie, it's me, Drayton Carlisle.'

Cass was flooded with relief. Briefly. Then she tensed again.

'I woke her, I'm afraid,' he continued. 'I wasn't sure whether to lift her.'

He spoke softly, an apologetic note in his voice that Cass had rarely heard. Their relationship had always been too volatile for civilised exchanges.

'It isn't Melanie,' she announced and left him to play guessing games while she finally went to pick up her niece. ''Sa'right, I'm here. 'Sa'right. Shh,' she crooned, holding the baby into her body.

'You!' Dray Carlisle exclaimed, and reached to switch on a bedside lamp.

'Yes,' she confirmed as light filled the darkness, 'me.'

'I don't believe it!' he added, though he obviously did—and was less than thrilled about it. He took a step towards her, demanding, 'What are you doing here?'

'Right at the moment, trying to get Ellie back to sleep,' she responded as the baby's cries escalated. 'Unless you'd like to do it? In which case, could I suggest a slightly less aggressive tone?'

She offered the baby to him but it was purely a mocking gesture.

His eyes bored into her as he responded, 'Very funny...
I'll wait outside.'

'If that's what you want.' Cass's tone was dismissive.

'No, what I *want*,' he ground back, 'is to go to bed.'

Cass shrugged. She wasn't stopping him.

'Don't worry, that wasn't a proposition.' He crossed to the
door. 'After a nine-hour flight, I haven't the energy.'

'I wasn't worried,' she returned sharply.

It backfired, however, as he paused briefly in the doorway
to murmur, 'Now that *is* interesting.'

'I didn't mean—' She tried to correct any false impressions
but he was already walking up the corridor. She pulled a face
instead, reassuring herself that he *had* known what she'd
meant. He just enjoyed making her feel uncomfortable.

Of course it now seemed like an act of total lunacy. To be
here in his house without permission, nursing this baby, perhaps *his* baby, and putting herself in this vulnerable position.
She must have been crazy!

She went on pacing the floor, a manifestation of nerves,
but at least Ellie found it soothing. Her cries gradually subsided to the occasional whimper, then transformed into snuf-
fling as her breathing levelled out.

Cass carefully laid her back in her cot and switched off
the light, but she was in no hurry to leave the room. She sat
in a rocker in the darkness and counted the minutes going
by. Ten, fifteen, twenty—was that long enough?

There was no sound from the corridor. Had he lost patience? Had he gone down to his own floor? She waited another five minutes to be sure, before slipping back through
the adjoining door.

She shut it firmly behind her before groping for the bed
and the lamp beside it. She almost jumped out of her skin as
she switched it on to find him sitting in an armchair in the
corner. It was creepy how he could be there, silent in the
darkness, without her sensing it.

He seemed quite relaxed, one hand in a pocket, the other nursing a glass, his long legs stretched out in front of him. He was still wearing suit trousers and a plain white shirt, but it was open at the neck, the tie two strips across his shoulders.

She remained standing, demanding rather fatuously, 'What are you doing here?'

'That's my line surely…I live here, remember?'

'I was told you were in America.'

'I realised that,' he drawled back, studying his fingernails. 'I presume you would not be enjoying my hospitality otherwise… How many days have you been here?'

She scowled darkly. He made it sound as if she'd been freeloading off him.

'I came this afternoon to see how the baby was,' she relayed. 'I had no plans to stay but Mrs Henderson's husband has broken his hip and there was no alternative.'

'What about Melanie?'

'She's walked out.'

His eyes reflected suspicion. 'I wonder what made her do that.'

'Don't look at me! I've never even met the girl… She was probably missing you,' she suggested somewhat unwisely.

His jaw tightened. 'And what's that supposed to mean?'

'Work it out!' Cass didn't hide her disdain.

A haughty stare was trained on her. She made the mistake of staring back. Their eyes locked for what seemed an interminable moment.

When he finally stood and crossed the room, she couldn't quite remember what they were arguing about.

'You think I was involved with her?' he asked in deceptively quiet tones.

Cass gave no comment rather than make things worse.

'You do, don't you? You have some absurd idea that I go around seducing any woman who steps into my path. You do have a low opinion of me…or is it of yourself?'

It was Cass's turn to demand, 'Meaning?'

'First you accuse me of sleeping with your sister and fathering her child,' he recounted, 'then imply I've moved on to the teenage nanny, whom, incidentally, I wouldn't know in a crowd. Is there anyone else you'd like to suggest? Mrs Henderson, perhaps?'

'Who knows?' she parried.

'Exactly—who *does* know?' He used the words against her. 'The general idea is I'm indiscriminate, yet what actual evidence have you? *Who* is the only person *you* can absolutely say for certain has been in my bed?'

It took Cass just a moment to catch on, then a dull angry red heightened her cheek-bones. He was talking about her, of course.

'Is that the logic, Cass?' he ran on. 'You're worthless so anyone willing to sleep with you has to be even more worthless?'

Cass didn't give his theory more than a second's thought before countering, 'That's the most absurd thing I've ever heard in my life! If I've slept with you—'

'No *if* about it.'

'All right, the fact I've slept with you, call it a moment's madness, an act of lunacy, but, the rest, that's just amateur psychology claptrap!' she dismissed contemptuously.

Cass didn't care if she provoked a fight. An angry Dray Carlisle she could deal with.

It seemed, however, he was working to a different agenda.

'Acts,' he eventually replied.

'*What?*'

'*Acts* of lunacy. More than one. Sixteen, in fact. Nineteen if you count oral sex.'

Cass was finally shocked into silence, both at his frankness and the idea that he'd kept a tally.

She waited for a mocking smile to appear, but he remained

deadly serious, his gaze willing her to remember how it had really been.

Cass remembered well enough. She didn't need steady blue eyes calling her back to that time. Even angry with him, she could still feel it—an attraction so primitive it threatened to overwhelm any other emotion.

Safer to take refuge in indignation, to raise her arm, to transcribe an arc to his cheek-bone.

He didn't expect it, but, in a way, neither did Cass. She'd never slapped anyone before. It was alarming, the cracking sound, the sharp hurting sting on her palm, his head jerking in recoil.

She saw the mark of her fingers on his cheek and, before he had a chance to react, she backed away from him. An arm went out to stop her and, panicking, she turned to run.

She never even made the door. He was on her, hand gripping her by the sleeve, pulling her round so roughly the shirt ripped and she spun backwards. She would have fallen had he not caught her. Gratitude, however, wasn't uppermost in her mind as he pinned her against the wall. She might have struck out a second time but his hands were now steel bands round her wrist.

'Let me go!' she snapped at him, furious rather than frightened.

'So you can hit me again? I think not.'

'You asked for it!'

He arched a brow. 'By telling the truth? Is it so hard to face—the fact we had sex together?'

Cass gave him a derisive look in reply and tried, unsuccessfully, to jerk her hands free.

'It shouldn't be.' His voice hardened. 'You knew the whole time, after all.'

'Knew what?'

'That we were having sex.'

Cass stared at him. He was making no sense, yet he expected an answer.

'What else?' she muttered back.

'What else?' His lips twisted at her words. 'You really had no illusions, had you? No thoughts that we weren't just *having sex* but actually making love. No plans for a relationship that would last longer than a couple of weeks.'

What was he saying: that *he'd* had such illusions, such thoughts, such plans?

She shook her head and he took it as his answer. 'No, of course not.'

'I never said—' Cass tried to backtrack.

He wouldn't let her. 'You imagine that makes things better? The fact that you said nothing?'

'You don't understand—' she appealed hopelessly.

'Like hell I don't!' His voice lowered to a harsh note. 'Oh, you said nothing all right. You waited until I was head over heels and making true confessions before you decided to walk. And even then you said nothing. You left your sister to do it for you!'

Cass stared at him in wonder. He'd been head over heels? He'd loved her as he'd claimed? Loved her as she'd loved him? Could it be possible?

Possible or not, it was in the past, dead and gone, as he growled at her, 'Don't give me that wide-eyed look! You knew how I felt. I practically went down on my knees to you, and still you said nothing…because that's what really turns you on, isn't it?' he demanded, dragging her body closer to his.

His breath was hot on her face like his anger and her arms were crushed against his chest. She swallowed hard, but no words came.

He didn't wait for an answer, anyway. 'That sense of power over me. It's what you taste when I kiss you. See.' He covered her mouth and kissed her hard, smothering any cry of protest, before continuing hoarsely, 'So how was it, Cass, sweet or bitter?'

Cass shook her head once more. She didn't want to go down this road. It was too dangerous.

'I have no power,' she breathed unsteadily.

'Haven't you?' He slid his hands down to her hips and pulled her lower body briefly against the hard pulse of his.

She drew back immediately and he let her, but only so far, before he lifted a hand to tilt her head.

Every alarm bell was ringing in Cass's head but when he asked, 'You're not scared, are you?' pride came before good sense.

'Why? Should I be?' She threw him a defiant look.

Mistake. Dark blue eyes met and held hers. She felt mesmerised by his gaze.

It took all her will-power not to tremble as a hand began to caress the nape of her neck.

'So cool and controlled—' His voice was admiring, but he was intent on destroying that composure.

She held her breath when his hand lifted to smooth back the hair from her face, then cup her cheek.

It was a contest of wills. Cass knew he was winning even before he traced the outline of her features and her heart stopped beating. He rested his fingers against her mouth and she gasped slightly, needing to breathe. It was what he wanted, access. The tips of long, tapering fingers slid in and out, moistening her lips as a kiss might.

Only somehow it was more intimate and she shut her eyes in reflex. *'Don't!'*

'I have to.' A whisper against her lips as he took her face in his hands and finally lowered his mouth to hers.

I can't. A cry in her head that was never uttered. And anyway it was a lie. She could. It was easy.

When it came to him, it was all too easy. He didn't have to force her. The first gentle touch of his lips and her resistance was minimal. For all of ten seconds, she was passive, then she was helplessly responding, clinging to him as he deepened the kiss until it was an intimate loving invasion that left her breathing hard.

He gave her no chance to recover as he pressed her against the wall and, with one hand still buried in her hair, began a slow journey down her body. He kissed her temple, lobes, the curve of her cheek, flicking with his tongue the pulse beating wildly at her throat. He pushed aside the gaping neck of her shirt until he could taste the sheen of perspiration in the hollows of her shoulders.

She was lost even before a hand slipped under her make-shift nightshirt, forcing buttons loose to expose the soft, rounded flesh beneath. He cupped the weight of her breast for a moment, then reached a thumb to stroke the nipple. She moaned aloud and he dragged her head back and stifled the sound with his mouth.

He kissed her hungrily, with lips and tongue and teeth, while his hand moved between breasts, gentle at first, slowly fingering, then pulling, tormenting, until the peaks were swollen hard and she was weak with longing. They swayed towards the narrow single bed. She fell with him and lay under him, a willing victim, as he tore open her shirt to put his mouth to her breasts, sucking and biting and playing, while a hand smoothed over the flat of her belly downwards to the soft, secret place between her thighs.

It was true. He had forgotten nothing. How to touch her, to stroke her, to draw the small pleasure noises from her mouth until she was aching for him, arching to him, needing completion.

Only when he raised his head away did Cass hear another sound: the crying of a baby.

Dray gave a low groan. He'd heard it, too.

'Ignore it…just for a little.' It was a plea not a command,

as he entwined his limbs with hers and began kissing her again.

Cass tried. She still wanted him. That didn't change. But as the crying grew louder, it also grew harder to block.

'I'm sorry,' she finally murmured against his mouth, 'I can't.'

He lifted his head once more and saw her distracted look. He swore in frustration, but muttered a resigned, 'I understand,' as the baby's crying rose another pitch.

He rolled away from her and, sitting on the edge of the bed, watched as she buttoned her nightshirt. She was all fingers and thumbs, made worse by the fact that he was still stroking her thigh. She raised her head to find him smiling.

He knew the effect he had on her. She'd made it fairly obvious, after all. This was just an interval.

Half dressed, she hurried through to the nursery to pick up a distressed Ellie. She imagined he would stay in the other room, but he didn't. He followed her through, and switched on the softly glowing nightlight. It seemed he didn't want to let her out of his sight.

His eyes rested on her as she paced the floor, holding Ellie to her warm body. She tried to keep her thoughts focused on the baby but it was hard. She was still light-headed with desire for Dray.

When Ellie was near to sleep again, she laid her in the cot and they both stood for a moment, looking down at the pouting mouth and the flutter of long lashes on soft, rounded cheeks.

'She's rather beautiful, isn't she?' he said softly.

'Yes,' Cass had to agree.

'Maybe that will make a difference,' he added in the same musing tone.

Cass understood what he meant. Beauty could open doors, hearts even. His words, however, brought a sudden chill to hers, as the reality of their situation surfaced once more.

'Why?' Her gaze went from the baby to the man, kin t
each other in their dark good looks. 'Does it to you?'

Her voice was low so as not to waken the baby, but th
note of accusation in it couldn't be missed.

When he raised his eyes back to her face, it was with
quizzical expression.

Had he imagined she was suddenly tame? A little love
making and she'd forget his own role in the whole sorr
business? Did he think her so weak?

He was silent for a moment, eyes burning into hers, read
ing her mind.

'You still think she's mine?' he challenged in low tones.

There was an undercurrent of anger in the question. I
would have been easy to take it as a denial. But wishing
thing so didn't make it so. Cass had learned that a long tim
ago.

'Well, she isn't,' he added unequivocally.

Now that *was* a denial. Nothing open to interpretatio
about it. She could fall right back into his arms.

That was clearly what he thought, at any rate, as he cam
round the end of the cot and reached for her.

Cass, however, was already backing away, determined no
to let him touch her. If he did, she'd be lost again.

'You must think I'm a fool,' she flashed at him, 'to tak
your word, just like that, so I'll go back to bed with you.'

It stopped him in his tracks. His hands fell back to hi
sides and the half-smile on his face became a thin, angr
line. He didn't like being called a liar.

'No, I think you're a coward,' he eventually mutter
back, 'hiding from the truth and your real feelings, cravin
intimacy yet scared of it, running from anything or anyon
you can't handle.'

Just words. So why did they hurt so much? Because the
were meant? Because they rang true? Or ultimately becaus

he was the one to walk away, turning on his heel, leaving the room and her without a backward glance?

All these and more, Cass realised as she went back through to the bed where they'd almost made love and lay down on it, and curled into a wretched ball, and tried desperately to ignore the longing eating at her inside.

CHAPTER EIGHT

WHAT happened the following day wasn't planned. Cass's last thought on falling asleep and her first thought on waking was how quickly she could leave. Only the needs of a crying baby stopped her going immediately.

She went through and picked up Ellie, continued on to the bathroom where she dressed before going downstairs. There was no sign of Dray Carlisle and, at first, she was relieved. She made up a feed in response to Ellie's hungry cries and sat nursing her in the kitchen, memorising the detail of her face and hair and little hands, believing this would be their last meeting for a long time.

When the baby fell asleep again, Cass laid her in the pram, fetched her coat from the back door and sat, waiting for Dray Carlisle to appear. She assumed that, jet-lagged, he was still asleep upstairs.

The minutes ticked by and the ringing of the phone finally disrupted her solitude. She left him to pick up on a bedroom extension, but it kept ringing and ringing until she had to answer or risk waking Ellie.

'Cass?' enquired a familiar voice and, for a mad moment, she imagined he was ringing from upstairs, checking if she'd gone.

'Yes,' she said at length.

'It's Dray,' he added, unnecessarily.

'Yes,' she repeated.

A deep sigh was drawn on the other end of the line before he asked, 'Did you get my note?'

'Note?' she echoed.

'You didn't,' he concluded. 'I put it under your door.'

When? Cass wondered, closely followed by, Why? Did he dread the idea of another meeting so much?

'Where are you?' she finally thought to ask.

'Work,' he answered succinctly. 'I had an eight a.m. meeting I couldn't cancel.'

Forget the fact he'd been up till two. Or the fact he'd just flown back from America. Or the fact he'd dumped her with a baby that wasn't *her* responsibility.

'Don't worry,' he went on, reading her mind, 'relief is on its way. The agency is supplying emergency cover.'

'What agency?'

'Nannies UK. They're sending a girl over immediately.'

'R-r-r-ight.' It was a drawn-out right, one that clearly meant the opposite. 'And you expect me to interview her.'

'What?' He'd clearly never considered such an idea. 'No, of course not. The agency has already checked her references. All you have to do is hand Ellie over.'

Like a parcel, Cass thought as she muttered back, 'Should I get the girl to sign for her, perhaps?'

'Sign for her?' Irritation crept into his voice. 'If you want; though I'd hardly say it was necessary. Look, I'll speak to you later. I have to go and—'

'Well, don't let me keep you!' she cut in and replaced the receiver abruptly.

She was walking away from the phone when it rang again. This time she ignored it which wasn't perhaps the most sensible thing as it rang and rang until Ellie woke, crying. She still ignored it and, picking up the baby, went for a walk round the house.

North Dean Hall had been in the Carlisle family for four generations but dated further back than that. Its large, high-ceilinged rooms spoke of an era when there would have been an army of servants waiting on one family, rich enough to have as many children as nature allowed. There would have

been soirées and parties and dancing, the sound of laughter
chasing down the corridors.

Now it was so empty she felt that if she laughed, it would
echo off the walls and crack in the oppressive silence. Dray
Carlisle chose this splendid isolation but what about Ellie?
Would she be lonely in these endless rooms? Would she feel
unloved, forgotten? Or would wealth make up for it all?

Cass didn't have any answers. She just knew that when
the nanny arrived—a young nervous girl suffering from a
very heavy cold—this life wasn't good enough for her niece.
She sent the nanny away, made a phone call, went upstairs,
packed some essentials in a holdall and prepared two milk
feeds for the journey. By the time the taxi arrived, she was
ready.

She didn't allow herself to think about what she was doing
until she was on the train to London and by then it was too
late. She didn't examine her actions too closely but concentrated on taking care of Ellie. She hadn't realised the hard
work involved in coping with a very young baby, public
transport and all the paraphernalia required.

When she finally reached her local station, she was exhausted from folding and unfolding a pushchair while jug-
gling a baby and a holdall. She felt a measure of relief when
a fretful Ellie fell asleep on the way to the house.

She let herself in with her key and carefully manoeuvred
the pushchair over the front step and into the hall. She left
her there while she emptied the holdall's contents—nappies,
wipes, and a change of clothes, milk powder and a compact
sterilising unit—on the kitchen table.

She had no cot, of course, or toys, or mobile or any spare
money to buy such things. She looked round the shabby
house that had never really felt like a home and had to remind
herself why she had rescued Ellie in order to take her to this.
She had to visualise the sniffing nanny, a girl scarcely out of

school, and the utter indifference of Dray Carlisle, a man who spent his life scrupulously avoiding marriage and babies.

At the same time, a voice was muttering in her ear, listing the things she'd cost her niece—the twenty-room mansion in Berkshire, the private education, the toys and clothes and presents, all compensation, surely, for her motherless state.

'Those things aren't what's important,' she said aloud but could hear the lack of conviction in her tone.

For what had *she* to offer this baby? Love? She'd never been very good at that. Family? There was just her left and what if she died? A future? She could barely see past the next hours.

What *had* she done? Cass looked at her sleeping niece and it began to dawn on her. She hadn't thought it through. She had merely reacted, as she always did when Dray Carlisle was around. Now she would have to live with the consequences.

As distraction, she opened the mail she'd found lying on her mat but it only served to underline how far-reaching these consequences could be. Among the bills was a notification of the current state of her student loan and a letter from the general practice she was joining, detailing arrangements. The debt told her she had to work and the letter left her wondering how she could start, Monday week, in Slough, with a baby in tow.

She saw no easy way out. She'd worked hard to become a doctor but it was virtually impossible to be one *and* a single mother. It seemed it came down to a choice, the baby or her career.

She'd still not made that choice when dusk fell and there was an anticipated ring on the doorbell. She knew it was Dray before she pulled back the curtain. He'd already made an appointment of sorts.

He'd rung her at five and the briefest of conversations had ensued.

'Cass?' he'd said when she'd picked up the phone without speaking.

'Yes.'

'Is she there?'

'Yes.'

'Right.'

The receiver had been replaced, as if he hadn't trusted himself to say more. Cass was left to interpret that incisive 'right'. It was either 'right, that's fine, you keep her' or 'right, I'm coming to get her'.

There was no point in running. With infinitely more resources, he would catch her. So she sat waiting to see which it would be. She sat waiting, unsure which outcome she preferred until he arrived and she realised she'd been holding her breath.

She faced the truth. In a fit of conscience or madness she'd taken Ellie home with her. But did she really want to bring her up? All those years studying, struggling—and failing—to look after Pen, working in dead-end jobs just to get by. It had been no life. Did she want to repeat it—inflict it on somebody else?

No.

She scarcely reached the door when Dray rang the bell again. She opened it wide and allowed him to enter. He seemed taken aback. Perhaps he'd imagined he'd have to batter the door down.

'You've come for her?' she asked without preamble.

The scowl on his face deepened. 'What else?'

'She's through the back.' Cass went to fetch her.

A hand shot out to stop her. 'Hold on a moment.'

He gave her no choice. His fingers dug into her upper arm and betrayed barely controlled temper.

Cass remained cool in response. 'I don't want a fight.'

'You think I care what you want,' he grated back. 'It takes you two months to come see your sister's baby, then you turn up out of the blue and start behaving like you're Mary Poppins... Only it's all show with you and no substance, isn't it, because one short day and you've had enough?'

Colour filled Cass's high cheek-bones as she tried to explain herself. 'I know I acted rashly and perhaps you have the right to be annoyed—'

'*Annoyed?*' he rasped at her. 'Annoyed doesn't cover it! Annoyed doesn't even remotely touch it! What the hell were you playing at, sending that girl away—?'

'She wasn't suitable,' Cass interjected with a little of her normal spirit.

'Yes, of course,' he resumed, 'she didn't know how to perform a tracheotomy, did she? Or was it her inability to do cardiac massage?'

Sarcasm dripped from his voice as he put his own slant on her brief interview with the temporary nanny.

'I asked her what she'd do if Ellie was choking or stopped breathing, that's all,' Cass retorted in kind, 'and I think both are quite acceptable questions. The girl was also suffering from a very heavy cold and, in case you don't know, young babies are very susceptible to respiratory infections.'

'You sound like a walking textbook,' he accused, 'but then that's pretty much the extent of *your* knowledge of babies, isn't it?'

'No, actually it's not.' Cass had babysat for pocket money all through her teenage years.

His eyes narrowed on her face, suddenly suspicious. 'Was it true, then?'

'Was what true?'

'Your sister once implied you'd had a baby when you were a teenager.'

'She *what*?'

'You heard.'

Cass had heard all right. She just didn't credit it.

'Pen claimed I'd had a baby?'

'Not in so many words. It was a remark she made after you ended our affair.'

Cass wasn't going to let that pass. '*I* didn't end it!'

'No, you weren't that brave,' he threw back. 'It was Pen who explained that experience had given you a cynical view of men: that they have their fun, and the woman's left holding the baby.'

Cass frowned. She had said something like that to Pen years ago, but when and why had Pen relayed it to Dray?

'I didn't know if she meant firsthand experience,' he continued. 'By that time I didn't want to know.'

Because it had suited him, Cass assumed. He'd been ready to move on and had used a few careless words from Pen to give himself an excuse.

'I was never *your* sort, was I?' she accused now.

'Maybe not.' A shrug dismissed it as past and so irrelevant, yet he asked, 'Was there a baby?'

Cass's face suffused with colour, as she was torn between the truth and the promise she'd made to Tom, not to disclose Pen's earlier pregnancy.

'I'll read your silence as yes,' he answered for himself. 'So what happened to it?'

'*Him.* He died.'

She aimed for matter-of-fact but her voice betrayed her. She still felt grief for that first baby.

Dray heard it, too, surprising her with a genuine, 'I'm sorry.'

She shook her head. She didn't want his sympathy. It would be under false pretences.

'That's Ellie.' She was almost relieved to hear a demanding cry coming from the kitchen.

He was still holding her arm, but gently now, the thumb brushing absently against her skin. When she tried to pull away, he tightened his grip for a brief moment, as if he didn't wish her to go, but Ellie's cries rose, forcing the issue.

Released, Cass stood a moment longer, flustered by his steady gaze, then she turned and hurried towards the kitchen.

It was small surprise Ellie had woken. Cass had made a makeshift bed for her with a folded sheet in an open kitchen drawer, but it was hardly the soft luxurious cot to which she was accustomed.

Cass picked the baby up but she continued to cry, working herself into a state.

Dray Carlisle watched from the doorway. It was scarcely helpful. Cass was tempted to hand him the crying baby but she had little confidence he would do better.

Instead she trained herself to ignore him, and, cradling the baby's soft downy head in her hand, she rocked her gently until she eventually quietened.

'You make it seem easy,' Dray Carlisle remarked.

It could have been a compliment but Cass didn't want to take it that way. 'Have you brought a car seat for her?'

His brows drew together before he nodded. 'Why did you take her, Cass?'

He clearly meant why take her, then give her back so easily.

'I thought I could care for her,' she admitted, 'but I wasn't being realistic. I have a student debt to repay and, a week next Monday, I start my GP training. I can't look after her and work, and, if I don't work, would she thank me for taking her away from all the things you can give her?'

Dray's eyes rested on the baby, curved into her arm, now the picture of contentment.

'It's difficult to say what's best, long term,' he replied evenly.

'Well, in the short term, you'll have to get a nanny,' Cass advised. 'One who'll stay with her for her first years. She needs some permanency.'

'Granted—' he nodded '—but I've been holding off until Tom sorts himself out.'

'Tom?' echoed Cass. 'I thought he was out of the picture.'

His lips held the vestige of a smile. 'You preferred me as the villain of the piece, did you? Well, sorry to disappoint, but Tom is Ellie's father.'

'It's certain?'

'Absolutely—I have the DNA tests to prove it.'

Cass would like to believe it. She'd never wanted Ellie to be *Dray* Carlisle's.

'I thought Tom was refusing to be tested.'

'I persuaded him.'

His flat tone hid more than he was saying. Cass was left to wonder what persuasion techniques he'd used.

'Is he going to look after Ellie, then?'

'That remains to be seen. Tom associates Ellie with your sister and he's still convinced she was being unfaithful to him right up until the point she died.'

'And was she?' Cass willed him to tell the truth.

He was slow in answering. 'It's possible.'

Cass read it as a 'yes' and discovered that the truth really did hurt. She struggled to keep her emotions in check.

'Is there anything else you want to ask me—like who was the man, for instance?'

He was mocking her. They both knew the man's identity. He just wanted to twist the knife. Payback, perhaps, for the past.

She shook her head. 'No, I don't think so.'

His mouth thinned into a line. Had she spoiled his sport?

'Know it all, do you?'

'As much as I need to.'

Cass didn't want to hear details of his affair with her sister. The fact of it was already painful enough.

'I've packed all Ellie's stuff,' she ran on. 'It's on the kitchen table.'

It was clearly a hint to speed up his departure but he seemed in no hurry to leave.

'And yours?'

'Mine?'

'Your things. You'll require some clothes, I imagine.'

'Sorry?' Cass felt she'd lost the place in this conversation.

'You'll be coming back to North Dean Hall,' he said in cool tones.

It was a statement, not a question. Did he really think he could dictate to her?

'Relax,' he added at her indignant look, 'it's to cater for Ellie's needs, not mine. Just until I can recruit another nanny. Assuming we can find one that meets your approval, of course.'

'*I* can't go with you,' Cass said at length.

'Why not?'

'Well, for a start, I have to pack up this place and move before I begin my new job.'

She also had to find a house to rent, a car to buy and some clothes to wear because, as a GP, she could no longer hide behind a white coat.

'Where is the practice?'

'In Slough.'

'That's commutable from North Dean. I have a little sports car you could use.'

Cass gave a dry laugh. Did he really think she wanted to turn up at her new work in a sports car? Wouldn't that go down well in the practice she was joining!

His motives eluded her, too. 'I wouldn't have thought you'd want me back in your house.'

'What *I* want is irrelevant,' he drawled back. 'What I've got is a small baby, no nanny and only the vaguest idea how to feed, bathe or change it.'

'*Her,*' she corrected, 'not *it*!'

'Okay, *her*—' he bowed to the criticism '—but the facts are the same.'

'What about Mrs Henderson?' she suggested the house-keeper.

'On leave till further notice,' he relayed succinctly, 'so, while you pack your bag, I'll take the baby's things out to the car and return with the car seat.'

Cass trailed him through to the kitchen where he collapsed the pushchair and shouldered the rucksack before returning to the hall.

Cass followed him back as far as the front door, Ellie still in her arms, and was waiting there when he returned with the baby seat.

'There's Camilla Carlisle,' she proposed with some desperation.

'There *was* Camilla,' he amended, 'until someone ruffled her feathers.'

'She was very rude to me,' Cass protested, 'although I don't suppose you'll believe that.'

'As a matter of fact, I do,' he declared to her surprise. 'Camilla had reasons to feel enmity towards your sister and I can imagine that feeling spilled over on to you.'

'I see.' Cass wasn't going to risk delving into these reasons.

'I doubt it,' he echoed dryly. 'However, if you'd like to accept the inevitable and go pack, I'll hold the baby.'

Cass could refuse. What could he do to her, after all? Nothing. But then it was what he *couldn't* do for Ellie that was at issue.

'I'll pack an overnight bag and stay for a day or two.' She offered the baby to him. 'Make sure you support her head.'

'I know that much, at least,' he replied, taking her.

One large hand cradled her head and neck, the other her body, but he kept her at arm's length, as if he was frightened of dirtying his clothes. It was not encouraging.

Cass hesitated only briefly before taking the stairs two at a time and hurriedly throwing some essentials in a bag. She heard Ellie begin to cry and the muffled sounds of a male voice, then silence. She sped back downstairs to find Dray pulling interesting faces for Ellie's entertainment.

He seemed quite relaxed and Cass wondered if he'd underplayed his baby-minding capabilities.

'Ready?' he said when he saw her.

'Yes.' She watched as he placed Ellie in her car seat and clipped her in.

He took her bag from her and, carrying it and the car seat, waited for her to precede him out of the house. He gave her no chance to close the door on him, had she wished.

Cass walked reluctantly down the path, then allowed him to lead the way to his car. This time it was a four-wheel drive. She climbed into the passenger seat while he stowed her bag and fitted the baby seat.

'Seat belt,' he instructed as he clicked his own into place.

But Cass was still having doubts. 'Look, surely there's someone else who'd help you care for Ellie. What about girlfriends?'

'Your sister's?'

'No, yours.'

'Mine?' He raised a quizzical brow. 'What makes you think I have a girlfriend, singular *or* plural?'

Cass wondered whom he was trying to kid.

'You're rich,' she replied bluntly. 'Rich men are never short of girlfriends.'

Dray's lips twisted slightly at the insult before he decided to pass it off.

'Well, I must be a sad case,' he drawled back. 'Stacks of money and *still* no girlfriend. Maybe I should take an ad out in the personal column: "Unattractive but extremely wealthy male seeks gold digger for insincere meaningless relationship." What do you think?'

Cass *thought* he was taking the mickey and didn't bother to reply.

It was he who concluded, 'No, on second thoughts, I've had enough of those to last a lifetime.'

His pointed tone told her that that was how he'd come to regard their affair.

Cass was still thinking of a suitable response when he suddenly leaned towards her. She flinched rather obviously and was left feeling foolish as he drew the seat belt round her and clicked it into place.

He waited until he'd pulled away from the kerb before commenting, 'If you suspect this is all part of a grand seduction plan, then let me disillusion you. I don't intend to leap on you the moment our niece is asleep. Last night was a…an aberration.'

'*An aberration?*' Cass was stung into retorting. 'Well, thanks, that makes me feel a whole lot better.'

His gaze switched momentarily from the road ahead. Deep blue eyes questioned the reason for her upset. Hadn't he just promised to be a gentleman?

'I can't do anything right by you, can I, Cass?' he said at length. 'Why is that?'

Cass shook her head, refusing to answer. How could she? Even she didn't fully understand her conflicting emotions.

After that conversation lapsed, each occupied by their thoughts.

Cass's mind stretched back to the end of their affair. It seemed almost as if he wanted to rewrite history, but events were surely indisputable.

They'd had a date mid-week to go out to a restaurant. She'd rushed home from day shift at the supermarket to shower and change. She'd been doing her hair when Pen had turned up, unannounced.

Just back from honeymoon, she'd hot-footed it into

London, demanding to know what Cass had been doing, dating her new brother-in-law.

Cass had been calm, almost indifferent, in the face of Pen's temper tantrum. By now her feelings for Dray had overridden every other consideration.

Pen had changed tack, switching to sisterly concern. She hadn't wanted to see Cass getting hurt. Dray Carlisle was all very charming but he had a low boredom threshold. It was almost a family joke—the fact he never stuck with the same girl for very long. Had Cass imagined *she* would be any different?

Cass had barely listened. She'd been so sure that what Dray and she had had together was special. When her taxi had appeared, she'd grabbed her coat and bag and left Pen to talk to thin air. Pen had called something after her, but she'd already been out of the door.

When Dray had failed to show at the restaurant, Cass had assumed at first that he'd simply been late. She'd waited and waited. An hour had slipped by. She'd sat in the bar area and watched the door until she'd finally had to accept he wasn't coming.

It had been only then she'd begun to wonder: had Pen been trying to tell her something? She'd gone home by train, her mind dwelling on Pen's words. It had been ten by the time she'd arrived at the house but Pen had still been there.

'Dray didn't turn up,' she said shortly. 'Has he called?'

'I'm sorry, Cass.' Pen grimaced. 'I was meant to pass on the message but you rushed off. Dray asked me to tell you he couldn't make it.'

'Oh, Pen!' Cass was a little cross, but relieved, too. 'Is he ill? Perhaps I should phone him.'

'No, he won't be there,' Pen relayed. 'He's gone away.'

'Away where?'

'To Paris.'

'On business?' Cass willed her sister to say yes.

Pen hesitated, then shook her head.

Cass read sympathy in Pen's expression and concluded, 'He's with someone else, isn't he?'

This time Pen gave a bare nod and Cass felt her world slowly implode. She didn't ask Pen for details, couldn't bear hearing them. When Pen said she was staying over, Cass went on up to bed, intent on hiding her feelings.

It was the first of many nights that she cried alone in her room. She was hollow-eyed in the morning, when she went to work.

Pen spent the next few days in London with her. Tom was abroad on a sales trip and she didn't want to go home to an empty house. Cass didn't feel much like confiding, not when she couldn't be sure that Pen would keep things to herself, but possibly Pen realised how upset she was. She behaved in an unusually considerate manner and as the weekend approached—a weekend off that Cass had been meant to be spending with Dray at North Dean—it was Pen who suggested Cass should go and visit their mother's cousin in Yorkshire.

Cass welcomed the idea of a change of scene and took holiday due to her. When she finally returned to London, she'd chalked Dray Carlisle up to bitter experience.

She didn't expect to hear from him again. Then, out of the blue, he phoned. It was two weeks after their break-up. She was still hurting but all her love for him had gone.

He said, 'Cass, we have to talk,' without the slightest sign of remorse in his tone.

She replied, 'No, we don't,' and put the phone down.

She wondered now if her refusal to speak was his reason for accusing her of ending their affair. Rubbish, of course. He'd ended it by going to Paris with someone else.

If she could just remember that—the pain and jealousy he'd caused her—she would surely be safe. For it wasn't something she ever wanted to relive.

She tore her mind back from the past and stared ahead into the night as summer rain beat heavily on the windscreen. She didn't realise they'd arrived at North Dean until he turned into the drive.

She half expected him to desert her the moment he'd carried the bags inside, but he didn't. He looked after Ellie while she made up some bottles in the kitchen, then he watched her give Ellie her final milk feed of the day.

Cass pretended to be unaware of him, even as she tried to guess what he was thinking. Was he asking himself how he'd ever become involved with someone like her? Or was he simply checking that she really knew how to care for Ellie? After all, she'd ostensibly had a baby, one who had died.

She wished she'd never allowed him to believe that, but it seemed too late to deny it.

'I'm going up,' she eventually said, unable to stand those penetrating blue eyes on her a moment longer.

'Goodnight.' He acknowledged her departure but made no move to follow.

It was a repeat of last night, bathing Ellie, getting ready for bed, lying in the adjoining room while her niece slept next door.

Only this time she lay awake, listening to sounds in the night, wondering if there'd be a footstep outside her door.

At first Cass imagined she was dreading it, but, as seconds turned to minutes then hours and she knew she was to be left alone, the frustration gnawing inside her told a different story.

Finally she stopped lying to herself and faced the truth. Three years ago she had loved Dray Carlisle. She had loved him despite every good rational reason not to. And three years on, nothing had changed.

She was his for the taking.

CHAPTER NINE

EXCEPT he didn't take her. He had every chance as her visit extended to one week, then two, while a permanent live-in nanny was sought, but it seemed that overnight he had lost interest.

It had to be one of life's little ironies: when she'd finally accepted that her feelings for this man were the same as they had been three years ago, he was suddenly impervious to her.

Perhaps she should have been grateful. Another affair might have left her more devastated than the last. But it was hard to feel grateful when, in keeping his physical distance, he also seemed to have undergone a personality change.

He was once more the Dray she'd fallen for, the man she'd found intelligent and witty and thought-provoking, the man who could make her mad and make her laugh almost simultaneously, who matched the strength in her character so she didn't have to temper it.

Of course she was suspicious. Why the change? Because he needed her, she supposed. He'd hired a temporary house-keeper and Jill, a mature children's nurse, to look after Ellie during the day, but night-times remained Cass's territory. Fortunately Ellie slept through or Cass would have never coped with the long, demanding days at the practice where she was training.

Cass could have walked out, of course. She'd already stayed longer than they'd agreed. The routine, however, suited her. It took less than an hour to reach work—not in the sports car, but a hatchback he'd rustled up from some-where—and she spent most days shadowing one of the senior doctors, an extremely pleasant woman who maintained enthusiasm for the job despite many years in general practice. Cass felt certain she'd picked the right career path and, though her days were busy, she still had energy in the evenings to bath and play with her baby niece before putting her to bed. Dinner she ate with Dray and they talked over their days like friends and the only problem she had was hiding her real feelings.

Meanwhile several nannies had been interviewed and none had proved suitable.

Well, that wasn't strictly correct. Dray had insisted Cass approve his choice and a couple had passed muster in her book, but, when it got down to it, *he* turned out to be the more exacting.

So far girls had been discounted as too talkative, too immature, too insipid and potentially too unreliable. It was gradually becoming evident that, as an employer, Dray did not suffer fools gladly.

'She's out,' he declared as they finished interviewing another potential candidate during Cass's afternoon off.

The girl, a twenty-four-year-old, showed every sign of being smitten, only not by Ellie, lovely baby though she was.

'Why exactly?' Cass wondered if he'd noticed the girl's attraction to him or had he another reason.

'She's too…' He searched for an appropriate word.

Cass hid a smile, prompting, 'Too…?'

'Lightweight,' he finally decided on.

'Lightweight?' What was he looking for in a nanny? He'd already discounted a perfectly pleasant young woman because she'd struck him as too intense. 'I thought you wanted someone with a less serious attitude to life.'

'Yes, well, there's a middle ground between frivolous and angst-ridden,' he responded dryly.

Cass agreed, although she wouldn't have called their last candidate frivolous, just a trifle gushy.

'So, let's see,' she reflected on his objections to date, 'we want someone young but mature, someone smart but not a clothes-horse, warm but not sentimental, responsible without being overly serious, and prepared to commit to an indeterminate length of service as a mother substitute for Ellie while retaining a certain amount of detachment and respecting your privacy within the household... Have I missed out anything?'

He heard the irony in her voice and it was a measure of their improved relationship that he chose to laugh rather than retaliate to the criticism.

'No, that about sums it up,' he confirmed with a slanting smile. 'You think I'm asking for too much?'

'Just a bit—' she nodded '—especially as you're not offering permanence of employment.'

'I can't until Tom decides what he wants to do.'

'True.'

Cass knew Tom had returned to work but he had yet to visit the baby whom he now knew to be his.

'When did he last see Ellie?'

'The day after she was born.'

'She may have ceased to be real to him.'

'Quite possibly...but he refuses point-blank to come here.'

Cass frowned. 'I thought you'd settled your differences.'

'Not altogether.' A brief hesitation followed before he admitted, 'Tom still imagines I had an affair with his wife.'

Cass's stomach curled into a knot. Lately she'd avoided thinking about this scenario.

'What about you?' He watched her closely. 'What do you think?'

Cass was no longer certain. She wanted to believe he'd never even looked at Pen but wanting didn't make it the truth.

'I don't know,' she said at length.

His mouth twisted. 'Still guilty until proved innocent. Well, don't expect me to mount a defence.'

Because he couldn't? Or wouldn't? Cass turned questioning eyes on him.

He met her stare, undaunted, and it was Cass who eventually looked away, scared of betraying her feelings for him.

He muttered something under his breath, then pushed back his chair. He'd crossed to the door before she realised his intention.

'There's still another girl to be interviewed,' she relayed.

'You do it,' he dismissed. 'I can't be trusted.'

'I didn't say—' Cass tried to backtrack but he'd already gone, closing doors none too quietly behind him.

Cass was left to conclude what she could from his reaction. He was either the world's greatest actor or he had never had an affair with her sister and his refusal to say so outright was merely a product of anger and pride.

Till then Cass had considered things from her own point of view. Once *her* lover, he had moved on to Pen. Jealousy had made her accept it as fact, from the flimsiest of evidence.

But this ultimate betrayal wouldn't be of her, but of his brother Tom. And how likely was that? The first time she'd ever met Dray Carlisle his concern had been for Tom and what kind of girl he was marrying. The second time had been at the wedding and, though he must still have had reservations, he'd put a good face on it for his brother's sake. He'd asked Cass to the funeral on behalf of Tom and made her stay for him, too. He had taken in Ellie and was still looking after her, albeit by proxy, until Tom got his act together.

It seemed he'd do anything to protect his younger brother, so why imagine he would dream of hurting him in this most painful of ways? Would Pen have been so irresistible?

Cass supposed that was why she was jealous. Common sense told her Dray Carlisle wouldn't have had some offhand affair with his brother's wife. If it had happened, it had been something deep and intense and unstoppable. *If* it had happened…?

That question rattled around in her head until the next candidate for nanny appeared—a definite maybe—and was still rattling around later when Dray telephoned.

'Dray, look, about earlier—' She wanted to make up.

But he was brusque and businesslike, cutting through her with, 'Tom's finally agreed to see Ellie. I'm sending a car. Could you or Jill bring her to the main office?'

'I...Yes, of course.'

'Good. The car should be there in half an hour.'

His tone was cool and distant and he rang off before she could speak again.

Cass might have felt sorry for herself, if she'd had the time. Instead it was a rush to help Jill, Ellie's nurse, wash and change the baby, and dress her in the cutest of outfits for this momentous meeting with her father. This preening left her a little out of sorts but ready for a nap, which she duly had in her car seat in the back of the company vehicle sent by Dray. Cass went with the baby as Jill had been promised an early finish that day.

Cass had never been to Carlisle Electronic Systems before. They were waved through a security checkpoint and drove up to a large modern office block of dark-paned glass. Beyond it lay the works, with original brick buildings jostling side by side with newer sheds of aluminium and steel.

Cass woke Ellie gently when they drew into a parking space; fortunately the brief nap had left her in a smiley mood.

Babe in arms, Cass followed the driver inside. He went past the reception desk without explanation but Cass was conscious of drawing curious looks. They proceeded along a corridor to a lift marked 'Private' which rose to the fourth floor, then walked out to a central area occupied by two women at desks.

One of the women dismissed the driver before buzzing through, 'Your guests are here, Mr Carlisle.'

'Fine,' was buzzed back, 'send them through, Joan, then you and Carol may finish for the day.'

This obviously came as a surprise to Joan and Carol, it only being three-thirty, but neither argued.

Joan came out from behind her desk, a smile encompassing Cass and the baby, and ushered her to a door marked Drayton Carlisle, Managing Director.

Cass found herself in a large office, its plate-glass windows giving a panoramic view of the site beyond.

The man at the desk stood, acknowledging her appearance with a slightly raised brow. 'I thought you might leave it to Jill.'

She shook her head. 'I'd promised Jill she could leave before four. Where is Tom?'

'In his own office.' He leaned forward to flick a switch. 'Tom?'

'Yes?'

'I have those figures ready.'

'Right, I'll come through.'

Dray clicked off the intercom switch before Cass had time to catch up with this conversation.

'He doesn't know she's coming, does he?' she concluded with some horror.

'If he did,' Dray drawled, 'I suspect he'd be making a bolt for the lift now.'

'Is this wise?'

'It's a high-risk strategy, I agree, but I think it's time things were resolved, one way or the other.'

He made it sound like business, pure and simple.

Cass had just time to figure out his current game plan. Reunite father and baby—or not, as the case might be. Either way, hand over the baton of responsibility to someone else. Thus dispense with any need to have Cass in his life.

The door opened behind Cass before she could ask him if that was it: his desire to get rid of her was really the driving force.

She turned with Ellie in her arms.

Tom had taken a couple of steps inside the office and now froze at the sight of them.

The initial expression on his face suggested that, at any moment, when he remembered how his legs functioned, he would turn tail and run.

But the horror gave way to fascination as he stared at the beautiful wide-eyed baby he'd last seen as a wrinkled scrap of less than thirty-six hours old.

Seconds ticked by in suspended animation, then Tom again looked ready to take flight and Cass shook herself into action.

She gave Tom no choice in the matter. She walked up to him and placed the baby into his arms. She held onto her until she was sure he was supporting his daughter properly, then took a step backwards.

For a moment he looked almost scared of the little bundle he was holding. Perhaps he had never cradled a baby before. But the shock on his face gradually changed to wonder.

When finally he smiled and, fortuitously, Ellie smiled back—she might have cried at this stranger—Cass had an overwhelming sense of relief.

'She's beautiful,' Tom remarked, still in a daze, and, after several more seconds, murmured, 'I didn't know.'

He could have meant, Didn't know she was beautiful, but Cass thought it went deeper: that he hadn't known he'd feel this way about her. It was quite obvious that Tom had just fallen in love with his baby daughter.

'I thought—' He shook his head but felt a need to explain to Cass. 'I was so angry, finding out about her other baby, one more lie on top of the rest she'd told me. It began to seem as if it were all lies. But *she* isn't.'

'No, she isn't,' Cass echoed the thread of hope in his voice.

'She's beautiful,' he said once more, then, choked with emotion, turned towards the door.

The baby was still in his arms.

Cass had an urge to follow but Dray was suddenly behind

her, holding onto her arm. 'Let him go. He needs to be on his own with her.'

Cass had realised that. It was Ellie's welfare which concerned her. But she allowed Dray to stop her and came round to face him, lightly pulling her arm from his.

'Are you sure?' she asked uncertainly. 'What if she cries?'

'Then he'll do what most men do,' he assured her dryly, 'and hand her back. Meanwhile, perhaps you'd like to enlighten me as to what Tom meant by *her other baby*. I presume he was talking about your sister.'

To lie or not to lie, that was the question. She'd promised Tom at the funeral but he'd just let most of the cat out of the bag.

'Yes,' she confirmed.

'And?' A black brow was raised.

'Pen had a baby,' she admitted flatly, 'an earlier one.'

Of course he'd already deduced that, as he asked, 'Was it put up for adoption?'

'No, that baby died.'

'The same as yours?'

Cass nodded.

'That's some coincidence.'

He caught and held her eyes. She managed to keep her gaze steady but a guilty tinge crept up her face.

'Boy or girl?'

'Boy.'

'Birthday?'

'The twenty-fourth of April.'

'And your baby's?'

'I—' Cass was loath to invent a date.

'Let me guess,' he helped her out, 'The twenty-fourth of April.'

'Yes,' she admitted at length.

'So,' he ran on, 'only one question remains—was he yours or hers?'

Cass saw no purpose in lying any more. Pen's reputation was already in tatters and Tom no longer seemed to care what Dray thought.

'Hers,' she said simply.

He nodded, as if that truth didn't surprise him, as if, indeed, it made more sense.

'Well, it's not hard to figure why she kept that quiet.' He sounded bitter but Cass didn't see why *he* should be.

'What choice did she have?' she threw back. 'You were scarcely keen as it was. If you and the rest of your family had known she'd had a child at sixteen, what chance would you have given her?'

He didn't argue the point, saying instead, 'But why make out you were the one who'd gone through such an experience?'

'She didn't exactly say that, did she?' Cass recalled. 'You were the one who jumped to conclusions.'

'Perhaps,' he conceded, 'but it was hardly surprising I couldn't think straight at the time. You'd just dumped me flat and left your sister to do the explaining.'

'What?' She wasn't going to let that pass. 'Hold on a minute. It was *you* who failed to turn up for our date, *you* who chose to go to Paris instead—and not alone!'

'There was a sudden crisis at our European headquarters.' He sighed heavily. 'Tom and I had little choice but to fly over. I imagined you'd understand—not use it as an excuse to go out with someone else.'

Cass stared at him in bewilderment. What was he talking about? There had been no one else. And Tom was meant to have been with him? But Pen had said...

That Tom was away on business, yes. But that Dray was with...there had been no details. Cass had just assumed...too much. And Pen had let her.

She shook her head, as she suddenly began to see the past rewritten before her eyes.

He misunderstood the gesture, saying, 'Don't deny it. I phoned late that night, I phoned the next day but you were still out. Pen tried to cover for you before coming clean.'

'I was there.' Cass was quietly insistent.

He gave her a look of disbelief. 'Like you were there all the other times I rang? Or on the Friday when I turned up in person and sat outside your door till one a.m.?'

'I'd gone to Yorkshire by then,' she admitted with a distracted air.

She was still struggling to take in her sister's part in all this. It seemed Pen had gone out of her way to ruin her relationship with Dray.

'*If* that was the case,' he grated back, 'why didn't your sister tell me as much? Why make me think you were off with some other lover?'

'I don't know,' Cass said rather weakly.

'Are you saying she lied?' He remained incredulous.

Cass didn't want to accept it, either. Of course she knew Pen had told lies, but she'd never imagined her sister had been capable of duplicity on this scale—and against her.

She ignored his question to ask instead, 'The things you said at the funeral—about my being promiscuous—did Pen really tell you that?'

He hesitated for a moment, before nodding. 'She made some oblique comments when she returned from honeymoon to discover we were dating but I didn't really taken them on board. It was only later when I'd gone to Paris and you'd disappeared that she decided to be more specific. She wanted to save me from making a further fool of myself,' he concluded bitterly.

Cass saw now: Pen had actually made fools of them both. They'd helped her, of course. She'd filled in Pen's silences and Dray had offered her a receptive ear.

'Are you saying she lied?' he repeated his earlier question.

She finally replied, 'Yes, totally,' but wasn't surprised when he continued to look sceptical.

'So why would she do that?' he added.

Jealousy? Was that it? Had Pen resented Cass succeeding with Dray where she had failed?

It seemed so terrible a reason Cass looked round for another, if only to give to Dray.

'Perhaps she was testing how tolerant you'd be to girls with a past,' she suggested, and her mouth twisted at the idea. 'Obviously you failed.'

'Did I?' he challenged in reply. 'I kept calling you right up to the day you put the phone down on me. I got the message after that.'

The wrong one, of course, but Cass didn't want to dwell on the if onlys. It would drive her crazy, imagining a future that might have been.

'Does it matter who did what to whom?' she said at length. 'You were never going to be serious about me. Not a shop girl, *a nobody*,' she threw at him.

'If I'd any bloody sense at all, I wouldn't have been!' he threw back.

'Well, there you are!' Cass thought she'd proved her point.

But he grated in return, 'Where am I exactly? Sitting outside your house like a lovesick boy, waiting for you to return from God knows whose bed.'

It seemed he still believed Pen's lies and Cass was already tired of telling him otherwise. It wouldn't change things, anyway.

'This is all past,' she dismissed and would have walked away if he hadn't grabbed her arm.

'Is it?' He pulled her round and, without warning, lowered his mouth to hers.

She was too startled to react at first, but, as the kiss deepened, demanding a response, any response, she felt a confusion of passion and anger that made her cry out in both pleasure and protest as her lips opened to his. Then she was in that lost world again, where time and place and differences meant nothing, and the only reality was the hands drawing her body to his and the hard hurting race of her heart.

His breathing was harsh when he finally raised his head from hers. He searched her face for the truth.

It was there, in eyes slanted with desire and lips parted with longing. She could hide it no more.

'Tell me it's past now, Cass,' he muttered low in his throat, knowing she couldn't.

He would have kissed her again and she would have let him but a door opened without warning.

It was Tom with Ellie in his arms. He looked from Dray to Cass.

Cass pulled herself free from Dray's embrace, although it was quite obvious what they'd been doing.

'I...um...sorry.' A surprised Tom kept glancing from one to the other, unsure how to react.

Cass finally recovered her wits, saying, 'Do you want me to take her, Tom?' and reached for a lightly crying Ellie.

He handed her over with some relief but his eyes followed the baby. It seemed an attachment had been made.

'I need a lift back to North Dean.' She spoke to Tom. 'Could you possibly drive me?'

'Yes, of course,' he agreed straight away, before referring to his brother. 'You don't need me for anything?'

'No,' Dray denied but his eyes were on Cass and they accused her of running from the situation.

Cass didn't care. She crossed to the door and escaped while she could.

She had to sort out her thoughts, ask herself what *she* wanted. She knew what he wanted. He'd made that abundantly clear.

'You and Dray,' Tom prompted when they were on their way to North Dean, Ellie strapped in the back, 'are you...?'

He tailed off and waited for her to fill in the appropriate word, but Cass wasn't sure of it, either. Not 'in love': that took two. 'Seeing each other'? Well, only because it was unavoidable at present. 'An item'? Hardly that. So what exactly?

'No,' she finally replied.

'Oh? I thought, when I came back...' He left it hanging again.

She shook her head. 'Just a quick visit down memory lane, that was all.'

Tom frowned before declaring, 'Of course! I forgot Dray and you were once...er...'

'Friends?' Cass suggested the euphemism while her tone revealed they'd been anything but.

'I never knew what happened there,' Tom ran on. 'Dray wouldn't talk about it and Pen just said you'd both woken up to how incompatible you were.'

Cass felt renewed anger. Pen, with her scheming, had been the one to give them a wake-up call.

Nevertheless she granted, 'She was right. We had—*have* nothing in common.'

Cass had to keep reminding herself of that fact. Wanting to go to bed with him was something else.

She put that out of her mind, too, and changed the subject. 'What are your plans—regarding Ellie, I mean?'

'I don't know.' He glanced in the mirror at Ellie in her baby seat. 'I'd like to have her home soon but I'm not sure how I'll manage.'

He sounded uncertain but Cass's hopes were raised. At least he recognised that home was with him.

'Do you have a housekeeper?' she asked.

'Not as such,' he relayed. 'Pen always preferred to have a couple of cleaners from town.'

'Well, it wouldn't be easy,' she continued, 'but with them

to look after the house and a nanny to look after Ellie, you *could* manage.'

'Yes, well—' he chewed on his bottom lip '—I'll have to see.'

He was obviously nervous at the prospect and Cass decided not to push him. His renewed interest in Ellie was enough for now.

When they arrived back at North Dean, she invited him inside and managed things so he held the baby while she made coffee and some milk for Ellie. He looked daunted when she handed him the feeding bottle but he soon got the hang of it.

She sat with him, sipping coffee and watching father and daughter get to know one another. It seemed Dray's high-risk strategy might have paid off. Clearly Tom was entranced with his baby.

It was into this scene of apparent domesticity that Dray Carlisle walked, but, if Cass thought he might be pleased, he certainly didn't show it. He refused her offer of coffee and left without another word.

Cass wasn't conscious of pulling a face at his back until Tom said, 'If he has a grievance, it's with me, not you.'

'With you?' Cass had understood that the grievances were Tom's.

'I…um…I thought for a while that he and Pen…' he hesitated to put it into words '…well, that they'd been intimate.'

'Yes, he told me.'

'Ridiculous, I know.'

Cass just stopped herself from saying, *Is it?* If Tom needed to believe otherwise, then who was she to disillusion him?

'I'm not sure he even liked her as a person,' Tom ran on, 'far less in that way. It was just a silly idea on my part because I thought Ellie couldn't be mine.'

He gazed down at his baby. She'd fallen asleep, sucking

the bottle, and now looked angelic. She was equally like both Carlisle men.

'Why did you think that?'

'Pen claimed the baby was due in mid-summer so when Ellie was born in May, full term, I began to wonder why she'd lied about her dates and why she'd kept the pregnancy from me for the first two months.'

'I can help you with that,' Cass put in gently. 'Pen came to ask me the medical risks if she had another baby. Unaware she was already pregnant, I advised her strongly against. She must have gone away and thought over her options before telling you.'

Tom nodded. 'I can see now that must be the case, but, at the time, I was questioning everything. When the doctor dropped the bombshell about it not even being her first pregnancy, it just encouraged my paranoia... Why had she kept that from me?'

'She thought you'd reject her,' Cass said simply.

He shook his head, even as he admitted, 'It made our whole marriage seem a sham. I asked myself why the lies about her due date, if this was my baby, and I remembered I'd been in America for a week round the time Ellie would have been conceived. I became convinced she couldn't be mine.'

Cass also wondered if it could have been an escape route. Pen's loss had rocked him to the core and there he was, left with the responsibility of a newborn. Perhaps denial had been his way of coping.

'Considering the situation,' Cass said at length, 'I don't think anyone blames you.'

His lips quirked downwards. 'Apart from Dray, you mean? When he brought the first test to me, proving she was a Carlisle, I was still so sure she wasn't mine that I actually accused him of fathering her,' he confessed with a shame-faced look. 'Dray didn't deny it, but then that's not his style.

"Never defend the indefensible or apologise for someone else's mistakes,"' he quoted in his brother's deeper tones.

'You mean he would react the same, guilty or innocent?'

'I suspect so. At any rate, all he said was "Get up, get dressed and get tested", then walked coolly out the door. We've barely spoken since.'

'He believes you still think that he and Pen had an affair,' Cass told him.

Tom emitted a groaning noise. 'I didn't realise. I *have* been avoiding him, but only because I feel such a fool over the accusations I made. I must have been mad to think it for a second. Even if he'd liked Pen, Dray is too decent to do that to me.'

Cass wasn't so convinced. With *her*, he'd never let notions of decency stand in his way.

'Perhaps I should go and speak to him now,' Tom said in resigned tones.

Cass made no comment. The thing between the brothers was their business. She just hoped that, if Dray had deceived Tom, it would be a truth that died with Pen.

'What about you?' Tom added.

'Me?' she echoed.

'I realise you can't stay here for ever,' he remarked, 'looking after Ellie.'

'No.' Cass suspected she'd already been here too long. 'I intend to go when a suitable live-in nanny's found. In fact, I interviewed a possible this afternoon... Maybe you'd like to meet her.'

'I...yes, I suppose I should. If you could arrange it?'

She nodded, but decided not to push it further for the moment. She didn't want to box Tom into a corner. He was clearly torn between paternal feelings towards Ellie and sheer funk at the idea of having responsibility for a small baby.

Still, she felt hopeful as he touched his daughter's soft

cheek with a finger, before handing her over, and he said goodbye with the words, 'See you soon.'

Cass saw him later, in fact, but only in passing. She'd gone upstairs to bath Ellie and prepare her for bed, when she glanced out of the nursery window. It looked onto the forecourt where Dray now stood with Tom. They were deep in conversation but Cass was too high up to catch it.

She couldn't decide whether they were quarrelling or making up until the moment of parting when the two brothers clasped each other in a hard male embrace and she saw the relieved smile on Tom's face. What Dray felt remained a mystery as his back was to her.

Cass returned to the business of settling Ellie for the night. She had her asleep by eight p.m., then with some reluctance went back downstairs. She didn't feel much like staging her own reconciliation with Dray but she hadn't eaten anything since lunch.

As usual the temporary housekeeper had prepared a meal. Sometimes they ate, side by side, in the kitchen. Tonight, a cold buffet had been laid out in the dining room. Cass was glad of the venue, because it was easier to maintain a distance in more formal surroundings.

Dray also seemed in no hurry to mend any fences. Having poured her wine, he sat to his meal at the opposite side of the table and lapsed into brooding silence.

The Cold War had returned. Perhaps it was just as well. She had grown too relaxed when he'd been civilised to her.

Now she was on edge once more, watching the scowl on that handsome face, waiting for it to be redirected from his food to her. For her own part, she found it easier to drink rather than eat.

When he glanced up, it was to observe her empty wineglass. He leaned across the table to refill it without comment.

Cass drank that second glass, too, aware it was going

straight to her head but not really caring. She felt a need to be anaesthetised to the whole situation.

'Another?' He held the bottle of wine to the neck of her empty glass.

'Why not?' She raised her glass slightly.

'Why not indeed?' he echoed on a hard note and, having poured the remainder of the white wine into her glass, got up to open a bottle of red stored in a cabinet. 'Let's you and I get drunk, then we can both blame the wine,' he added as he sat down again and filled up his own glass.

Cass could have ignored the remark, *should* have ignored it.

'Blame the wine for what?'

She gave him a stony stare.

He smiled back. However, it was a smile that never reached the eyes.

'For what's about to happen.'

Leave it, a voice of reason dictated but Cass was no longer listening to it.

'And what's that exactly?'

Cass had suddenly discovered a reckless streak of her own. Did she expect him to back down?

Of course he didn't. He wasn't the kind of man who did. Perhaps she hadn't wanted him to, either.

He barely paused before drawling back, 'Well, first we're going to fight a little because that's what we do and we're good at it, then we're going to make love because we both want it and we're even better at that... Or don't you remember?'

Cass remembered, all right. How could she not? He was looking at her as if he already had her undressed and in his bed.

She was shocked he'd been so direct but otherwise not shocked at all. Sex had been the driving force for their first liaison. Talk of love had just been an attempt to dress it up.

'No comment?' He arched a brow. 'Does this mean we can skip the fight part and go straight onto the main event?'

'No, actually it means—' Cass finally found her voice '—flattered as I am by such a romantic proposition, I think I'll skip that part, too, and go straight to bed... *Alone!*' she added hastily before he made any more of it.

She suited actions to words, and, pushing back her chair, made for the door.

She heard his chair scrape on the wood floor and an instruction to, 'Wait!' but she kept going, out into the hall and the stairs beyond.

By the time she'd reached the landing, halfway to the first floor, she realised he was following and it was already too late. She ran up the next flight and along the corridor to the door enclosing the attic staircase, but he caught her up and spun her round.

'Let me go!' she snapped at him, more angry than frightened.

'I will in a moment,' he promised, 'so there's no need to panic. I'm not about to do anything you don't want.'

That was the trouble—what *did* she want?

'I have to go and check on Ellie,' she insisted.

His eyes slid down to the waistband of her skirt. Clipped to it was the baby listener. Its lights were green, indicating no distress.

'Try again,' he suggested.

'All right,' she fumed, 'I have to get away from you before I do something we'll both regret.'

The threat hardly fazed him as he drawled back, 'I won't regret it.'

'I meant: slap you!'

'I know.'

'And that doesn't bother you?'

'Last time you slapped me, we ended up making love.'

It was statement of fact rather than boast, but Cass still railed against it.

'That was an aberration—your words—and it isn't going to happen again,' she retorted, jerking her arm free, 'so if that's all you want from me—'

'No, it's not *all I want from you*.' His mouth thinned to a line. 'If it was, don't you think I'd look elsewhere? You're not the easiest woman in the world, you know.'

'Really?' Cass scoffed at this remark. 'I was under the impression you thought the very opposite.'

'I was talking personality,' he countered, 'but, if you want to talk about the other—'

'Not particularly,' she cut in.

He ignored her. 'Then, yes, all right, perhaps I was a fool to believe your sister—'

'No perhaps about it,' she cut in again.

'But I wanted you, regardless. I wanted you even if you slept with every man you met. I went on wanting you long after you dumped me,' he admitted in a low tone fused with desire.

Cass was finally reduced to silence. Had he really felt so strongly? Had he hurt as she had?

'And I still want you, Cass,' he added unnecessarily.

Cass didn't doubt it, but she shook her head all the same. Wanting wasn't loving. Wanting was transient.

He lifted a hand and brushed her cheek with the back of his fingers.

A shiver of longing went right down her spine but Cass fought the feeling.

'Don't!' She took a step back from him.

His eyes creased at the rejection. Injured pride? What else?

'Why not?' he demanded unsteadily.

'*Why?*' she countered. 'Unfinished business?'

'What?'

'Is that all I am to you?'

'No,' he denied, 'and if you let me, I'll prove it.'

If she let him, he'd finally get over her, but where would she be? Lost for ever. Much better to break the spell now.

'You didn't like being dumped, did you?'

His face darkened, telling her she'd hit the nail on the head.

'Who does?' his voice harshened. 'You think that's what this is about? Getting my own back?'

He obviously didn't like her questioning his motives. Was she right? Were they reliving old times so Dray Carlisle could come out a winner this time?

'Well, if it is, there's no need,' she replied flatly, 'because I didn't actually finish with you, Dray. That was down to Pen and our own gullibility.'

He was silent for a moment, not comprehending. 'What are you saying?'

'Our last date at that restaurant,' she relayed, 'I went as planned. Pen only got round to telling me you'd gone to Paris when I returned home. At the same time she let me believe you weren't on your own—and no, I don't mean with Tom.'

'You expect me to believe this?'

'It's up to you but it's the truth.'

He remained suspicious. 'I called late that night. You still weren't home.'

'Yes, I was…I was upstairs.' She'd been upstairs, crying her eyes out.

He frowned in recollection. 'Your sister answered the phone and promised to have you call me. I phoned the next day and it was then she told me that you'd moved on to someone new. I thought she had it wrong. I was so sure I drove straight from Heathrow to your house and sat, waiting for you. You never showed.'

'I'd gone to a relative's in Leeds rather than sit around the house, moping,' she relayed, 'so you see, we're much in the same boat, imagining the other had dumped us.'

His eyes widened as he finally appreciated the fact that it had been Pen's deceit which had caused them to part first time round and none of Cass's doing.

'Why are you telling me this now?' he eventually asked.

'It's why you still want me, isn't it—' she held her head at a challenging angle '—the one girl who dared to end it before you did? Only I didn't. I was left hanging, just like you.'

I was left devastated, she could have said, but that was really her business. He knew enough to salvage his pride and walk away.

Somewhere along the line, however, she'd miscalculated, because, whatever reaction she'd anticipated, it wasn't a humourless laugh.

'You don't believe me?' She didn't hide her resentment; after all, she'd just bared her soul—well, half bared it, anyway.

'Actually, on balance I think I do,' he replied to her surprise. 'It's plausible, at any rate.'

'What's so funny, then?' she demanded.

'The idea that my wanting you is merely an act of revenge,' he returned, 'except it isn't funny. It's sad. That you have such a low opinion of yourself—'

'Hold on a second!' She hadn't told him the truth so he'd then go and psychoanalyse her. 'If that's a comment on anyone, it isn't me.'

'Isn't it?' He raised a brow. 'It couldn't be that I want you because you're the brightest, toughest, most real woman I know.'

'I—I...' Cass could think of no response.

It didn't matter. Dray needed no encouragement to continue.

'Or because each time you smile, a rare event, admittedly—' his lips quirked briefly '—I discover anew how beautiful you are.'

His eyes said he meant every word; they held her captive even as she shook her head. Then it was hands, reaching to clasp her waist and draw her to him.

'Or perhaps it's because I've spent night after night, imagining you naked, imagining touching your soft breasts, running a hand down your belly, hearing those little moans you give…' He trailed off, his breath a whisper against her cheek as he buried his face in her hair.

The tenderness of it overwhelmed Cass. Trembling, she heard the thunder of a heart beating hard—hers, his, the two as one? She shut her eyes but was still aware of the male scent of him. He pressed his lips to her temple. She finally surrendered to her emotions, and, turning, blindly sought his mouth with hers.

His kiss was all she longed for, all she feared. Desire was like the blood in her veins; it rushed too fast, making dizzy her senses, hurting her heart as only he could do.

Her head was already swimming, her legs fluid, when he picked her up in his arms and carried her to the nearest room.

His, of course.

CHAPTER TEN

HE STOOD her on the rug next to the bed. They were shadows in the half-light. He continued to kiss her hard, holding her head steady with one hand meshed in her hair, while the other unzipped her skirt until it fell to the floor. He drew her body to his. She felt his manhood rising against the softness of her belly. She trembled.

He began to drag down her tights. Any protest was stifled by the mouth still covering hers. She could only moan in her throat as a hand moved over her hips, exploring skin bared, sliding briefly, tormentingly, between her thighs.

When he finally raised his head away, she was mute. When he knelt to take off her shoes and tights, she was paralysed. He left her with just the thin barrier of bikini briefs.

He pressed his face to the V at the top of her legs and kissed and bit her gently through the silk until desire coiled and uncoiled like a snake and the intensity of it made her flinch. She grasped at his hair, but not to push him away. He was already moving, following his hands upwards, licking and kissing the flesh exposed as he gradually pushed up her sweater until, meeting no resistance, he pulled it over her head.

The cool of the night air touched Cass's heated skin but she was immune to it. She was like a doll, without a will of her own, waiting to be played with. She was perfectly compliant as he enfolded her in his arms and once more sought her lips with his.

Only now his kiss was an act of possession, raw and intimate, an invasion as his tongue entered her mouth like the thrust of sex, and she was shocked out of her passivity. She

171

whimpered aloud, clutching at his shoulders, digging into them as she unconsciously twined her body to his. He backed her towards the bed, a hard thigh parting hers. She closed her legs round it. He raised her hips and rubbed her body to his until she was warm and wet through the silk of her underwear and moaning her pleasure into his open mouth.

When he suddenly broke away from her, she thought for a moment that his sanity had returned, and she would go crazy. Then she heard the rustle of his shirt. He was unbuttoning it and she realised he was just slowing things down.

He took her hand and made her touch him, splaying her fingers out against his body. Heat rose from taut muscles. She stroked the damp hair on his chest. He moved her hand downwards to the buckle of his belt.

He wanted her to undress him. She understood. This was to be no seduction. She had to come to him willingly or not at all.

She could do no else. It was like a hunger. She hadn't known she had it. Now she was dying of it.

She unbuckled the belt with shaking fingers and tried to undo the top button. It was awkward or she was too nervous. Three years had passed since she'd last been intimate with this man.

'It's all right.' He touched her cheek with his lips and she sensed rather than saw the smile on his handsome face. 'I'll do it.'

He half lifted her onto the high bed and she leaned back against the headboard. He finished undressing. Her eyes had grown accustomed to the darkness and she could make out the shape of him, broad and powerfully masculine. If there was a moment to stop this, it was now.

But she said nothing. She had no use for words when their bodies could say it all. From the beginning it had been that way, from the day of her sister's wedding when, virtual strangers, they had come together on this bed.

He lay down beside her and drew her to him. He was totally naked. She hadn't realised. Hard flesh pushed against her thigh. The idea came to her that she wouldn't be able to hold him. Her mouth went dry.

He unclipped her bra and pulled a strap down one arm to expose her breast. She held her breath as the back of a hand lightly brushed against a nipple; she gasped aloud as he took it in his mouth. Tongue and lips and teeth licked and tasted and bit on her swelling flesh while she raked her nails on his shoulders.

He serviced both breasts until she was writhing beneath him, then he moved a hand down to the flat of her abdomen. It slipped between the silk of her briefs and her skin and reached for the warm, damp centre of her desire. He parted the wet, swollen lips and slid a long finger inside her and she shuddered against it, her muscles in spasm. Instinctively she drew her legs up against this intrusion.

'Shh. It's okay, okay,' he whispered in the darkness, 'I won't hurt you.'

He made soothing noises even as his fingers began to stroke deep and slow inside her, and she wanted to cry: not hurt her? How could he do anything else? Her body was on fire for him, beyond physical pain, but her heart would do the suffering.

Yet she didn't call a halt. She couldn't. She needed this as she needed food and drink to live.

She lay there, letting him touch her in ways no other man had, moaning with the long-forgotten pleasure of it, urging him on until the thrust of his fingers was so strong she almost came round them.

He stopped just in time and left her hanging there, on the edge, while he straddled her, then he grabbed both her hands and held them above her head as his mouth slid down her front to once more suckle her nipples, leaving her aching for the full act.

She arched her hips to his and finally, without warning, the full length of him entered her. Her first cry was startled, half pleasure, half pain, before it all returned to her. How he filled her, every part, how he moved, hard and powerful, how it felt, rising to meet each shaft. And how perfect it was, making love with this man, how unbearable, a sweet agony as she wrapped her legs round him and he drove into the core of her until they both fractured in ecstasy.

Still they didn't talk. They lay there, catching their breath, thoughts too fragmented for words, and, when they eventually turned to the other, it was to make love again, slowly this time, then fast and brief, and once, with an edge of desperation, as if it might be the last chance.

When dawn eventually crept through a gap in the curtains, it was Cass who woke first. She gazed at the man on the pillow beside her. She tested her heart and found it doing acrobatics. Last night hadn't cured the illness, just made it worse.

He opened an eye and caught her watching him. He smiled languorously, last night obviously on his mind, too. He reached for her but she sat up, away from him. There was no longer the cover of darkness to hide her feelings for him.

'What's wrong?' He caught her arm before she could move away. 'Don't tell me you're having regrets?'

She shook her head. Her only regret was loving him too much.

'I'd better see if Ellie's all right.' It was a patent excuse to get away.

It hadn't worked last night and it didn't work now. He leaned across her to pick up the baby monitor from the bedside cabinet. The green lights were on, showing the battery was still active. The absence of red lights and any sound indicated that Ellie was still asleep.

'She's fine,' he reassured.

'Look,' she tried again, 'I don't want to argue—'

'Good,' he cut in and, looping an arm round her neck, kissed her hard on the mouth, 'because I can think of much more interesting things to do.'

So could Cass and that was the trouble. One night and she was in danger of being enslaved again. She remembered the pain when she'd lost him three years ago. She had to protect herself.

'I can't do this, Dray.' Her eyes appealed for him to understand, to let her go.

He realised she wasn't talking about making love. They'd done that virtually all night.

She clutched a dislodged sheet and tried to slide out of bed but he held her fast.

'Do what?'

'Get in too deep.'

'Too deep?' An edge had crept into his voice.

'Emotionally,' she added lamely.

For a moment he looked stricken, then his face became a mask of anger, and Cass was left thinking she'd imagined his first reaction.

'So what was last night about?' he demanded. 'Just sex again?'

'I—I…' Cass took the easy way out, lowering her eyes as she agreed, 'I suppose so, yes.'

She didn't witness his reaction this time. She felt it as long tapering fingers crushed the bones in her arm before suddenly releasing her.

'Then go—' his voice was now a harsh whisper '—get the hell out!'

She heard his pain. It matched her own. But hers came from love whereas his…

She raised her eyes back to his but he was already turning away from her, drawing back the cover to swing his legs out of the bed. He didn't bother with clothes. It was a short walk to his *en suite* bathroom. He'd closed and locked the door behind him before Cass had time to reply.

She was effectively dismissed.

Initially she was too shaken to move. She'd felt a need to escape but now he had opened the cage, she no longer wanted to fly away.

What had she done? If she'd kept quiet, they might have had weeks, months, even a year together. That was better than nothing, surely?

She'd decided, yes, when she heard the shower going. He was washing himself clean of the smell of their love-making. He'd forgotten her easily last time. It seemed he would forget her easily now. Didn't that tell her everything?

She felt tears begin to slip down her face. She heard the shower stop as suddenly as it had started and that gave her the impetus to move.

She wrapped a sheet round her nakedness and retrieved her clothes from the floor before making a bolt for upstairs.

She was still using the nanny's room next to Ellie's. There was no sound from the baby yet, so she did as he had and took a shower, before dressing in jeans and T-shirt. She placed her luggage holdall on the bed and emptied her underwear drawer.

She got no further. The tears started again and, blinded, she sat on the window-seat. It wasn't a matter of having nowhere to go; she could easily find a bed and breakfast in Slough. It was finding the will to leave.

The door opened and closed behind her. She didn't turn. She knew it had to be him. She thought he would go away if she didn't speak but he crossed the room.

She pressed her face to the window-pane but couldn't hide her tear-stained face.

'You've been crying.' He sounded surprised.

Cass took refuge in anger. 'Full marks for observation, none for sensitivity.'

He didn't rise to the bait, adding simply, 'I don't understand you.'

That made two of them but Cass didn't want to try analysis.

'You shouted at me,' she offered by way of excuse.

'You dumped me,' he pointed out in return.

'It wasn't like that,' she insisted, weary of telling him this.

'Wasn't it?' He scrutinised her tear-stained face. 'It certainly felt that way.'

'I explained the past,' she reminded him.

'It's last night I'm talking about,' he countered. 'When are you planning to explain that? In another three years if our paths happen to cross?'

Cass felt her throat tighten. She didn't want to go through with this. She didn't want to walk away from this man. If she did, a lifetime of regret would follow.

'It wasn't just sex. It was...'

Love. She couldn't say the word. He would laugh in her face. But she had to say something to repair the damage between them.

He waited. He wasn't going to make this easy for her.

'I do have feelings for you,' she admitted almost formally, 'and I would like to pursue the relationship for a while.'

His brows drew together. He hadn't anticipated this volte-face. 'Define a while.'

'What?' She blinked at his businesslike tone. 'I—I don't know. A month or two. Longer, perhaps.'

'Be specific,' he said with the same steeliness.

'How can I?' She wondered what he expected.

He told her. 'Name a date.'

'A date?'

'When you intend leaving.'

Cass stared up at him. Was he joking?

'I need to know,' he added, deadly serious.

'Why? It's odds on you'll leave me first.'

'No, I won't.'

He said it as if it was a simple, inconvertible truth, but Cass couldn't see how he could be so certain.

'Is this some kind of game?'

'No. Why, is it to you?'

'No... Is it because of Ellie?'

'Ellie? What has she to do with anything?'

'I won't leave you in the lurch with her,' she promised, 'if that's what's worrying you.'

'Ellie doesn't come into this,' he denied. 'Tom will be taking Ellie home as soon as he can find suitable childcare.'

'Oh, that's good.' She was genuinely pleased for father and daughter.

'Do you really imagine that's why I've kept you around,' Dray continued with an edge of exasperation, 'as a cheap alternative to a night-time nanny? I can afford a professional for that.'

And for pretty much anything else, Cass supplied the unspoken words for herself, and felt a little foolish.

Dray reached down and, taking her hands in his, he drew her to her feet. He held her at arm's length as he told her, 'I want you to stay for me.'

It cost pride to say, and the pulse at his temple betrayed feeling. Did it matter if it wasn't love?

'Then I'll stay,' she echoed him.

He smiled but only briefly. 'I still need to know how long.'

Cass shook her head in frustration. They were going round in circles.

'But, Dray,' she appealed, 'I'd just be plucking a date from thin air and it wouldn't mean anything. This isn't business, with contracts that people can be held to.'

She was trying to talk sense but it prompted the opposite reaction.

'We could make it like that. We could make it exactly that. A contract.'

'A contract? What kind of contract?'

'The obvious kind when two people commit to staying with each other.'

'Are you talking about…?'

No, he couldn't be.

'Marriage.'

Yes, he could. Yes, he was.

'This is crazy!'

Cass's response had his mouth going into a rigid line.

'Why?'

'Come on, Dray. You and I, marrying—it just is.'

Cass was surprised he even needed to ask. She wasn't trying to offend him. She seemed to be succeeding, however.

'You think we're so incompatible?'

'Of course we are. Let's face it. You're rich, I'm poor. You're…'

Cass meant to make a list but ran out after the first item.

He raised a slightly mocking brow and she added rather lamely, 'We're hardly suited.'

'Because I'm rich and you're poor? Is that it?' It did sound a pathetic excuse the way he said it. 'Well, does it matter? Marry me and you'll be rich, too.'

'You think I'm after your money?' Cass was stung.

'Of course not.' He sighed in reply. 'I was merely stating a fact, that it wouldn't be to your disadvantage.'

'And what do you get out of it?' She couldn't see it would be to his advantage to marry her. 'I'd not be much asset as a corporate wife and my housekeeping skills are minimal.'

He thought briefly before replying, 'Good company, great sex, and a couple of children if things work out.'

Cass still wondered if he were joking but no laugh followed. She'd asked him a question and he'd answered it. It was not what she'd expected.

'You want children?'

'It's an option.'

'With me?'

'That's the general idea. When you're ready, of course. I realise you have a career to establish.'

It seemed as if he had it all planned, but Cass was struggling with the notion he'd want to marry her, far less have her bear his children.

'So, what do you think?' he added at her growing silence.

Cass thought that he'd taken leave of his senses. Or maybe she had, even hesitating. Perhaps she should march him to the nearest church and hope for a happy ever after. The trouble was, even in love, she was a realist.

'Isn't this all rather impetuous? We've only spent one night together.'

'I imagine I can trust my own judgement without needing a lengthy courtship,' he claimed with a touch of his more usual arrogance. 'I'm thirty-six, I run a fairly successful business and I've been with a wide and varied collection of women—your sister *not* included.'

Cass blushed at the final comment, accepting how foolish she'd been on that score.

He gave her a testing look. 'You do believe me, I hope. Even if I'd found her attractive, I would never have gone with my brother's wife.'

Cass nodded. She appreciated that now. Jealousy had affected *her* judgement. It was a destructive emotion that made people act badly.

She thought of Pen and the lies she'd told to keep her apart from Dray. Quite terrible lies. They'd come from jealousy. Perhaps Pen had regretted them, had really meant that 'Sorry about the Dray business' in her final letter, but Cass wasn't quite ready to forgive her.

'Pen found *you* attractive,' she told Dray now.

He shrugged in reply. 'Not as attractive as she found our cousin.'

'Your cousin? You mean Simon?'

'The same.'

'He was the one she…?'

Dray nodded. 'I had some suspicion and he confirmed it. He feels awful about it now but, at the time, he was quite besotted with your sister. I imagine she came as light relief after years of being married to Camilla.'

'I'm still surprised. I wouldn't have picked Simon as Pen's type, at all.'

'Perhaps she just liked the attention.'

It was a fair suggestion. It seemed Dray had understood her sister quite well.

'I'm really sorry—' she closed her eyes briefly in shame '—the things Pen did to your family.'

Dray gently squeezed her arm. 'Come on, it wasn't your fault.'

But Cass saw it differently. 'I should have tried to stop her marrying. I knew she was too young for commitment.'

'And you?'

'Me?'

'Are you too young?'

'I was never young. That's what Pen used to say. Old maid material from the word go.'

Cass relayed this without thinking. It had actually been a joke between Pen and her and she tried to laugh it off now, but he didn't laugh with her.

'You won't be if you marry me,' he pointed out in all seriousness.

'Is that a good enough reason?' Her eyes told him it wasn't.

Recollections of Pen's marriage made her realise none of the reasons he'd given would compensate for lack of the most vital ingredient.

'Perhaps not,' he conceded, thinking on the same lines, 'but I believe, in time, if you give it a chance, love would come.'

The word 'love' seemed strange on his lips, yet he'd used it once before to her.

That love, assuming it had been real, had long since died. Could she take a lifetime of waiting for it to grow again?

Cass shook her head. She wanted no illusions between them, no false promises.

'Love is either there or it isn't. I don't think you're going to wake up one morning, Dray, and discover you're in love with me. I don't believe it happens that way.'

Cass knew it didn't. She'd loved him three years ago, she loved him now, she'd never stopped loving him. Only pain and pride had masked it for a while.

'You missed the point,' replied Dray. 'I wasn't talking about me.'

'You weren't?' Cass frowned. He was right. She had missed the point.

'I already wake up every morning in love with you,' he told her quietly. 'I thought you understood that.'

Cass looked stunned. He was wrong. She had understood nothing.

'You're in love with me?'

He couldn't be.

'Isn't it rather obvious?'

Not to Cass. Not even now. He sounded more irritated than anything else.

'I... But...the way you've been over the last few months.'

'It was hard—meeting you again, discovering my feelings were still raw.'

'And after Pen's funeral,' Cass recalled, 'you couldn't wait for me to be gone.'

'It alarmed me how easily I'd lost control,' he admitted. 'I thought I was immune but I wasn't. I decided to keep away for my own self-preservation, but when your sister's letter turned up I wanted to test my reaction again.'

'You were very rude,' Cass reminded him but there was a

smile in her voice and her heart suddenly felt light enough to float away.

'I was very jealous of your doctor friend,' he grimaced back.

'There was no need to be,' she confessed in turn. 'Not of him or anyone else. One brief, failed affair, that's all I've had since you, and that was only for therapy.'

'Therapy?'

'I wanted to get over you.'

'And did you?'

She looked at him steadily, hiding nothing. He just had to use his eyes and see the naked love on her face.

Dray saw all right. Believing was the problem.

'Did you?' he repeated, needing to hear the words.

'I thought I had,' she ran on, 'but, after a brief remission, it turned out to be an incurable condition. I guess I'll have to manage it with regular intervention.'

It took Dray a moment to decipher this metaphor and his face moved between a frown and laughter, then back again.

'Bloody doctors,' he said in a half-growl. 'May I have that in plain English, please?'

'Yes, okay. I love you, Dray Carlisle. I loved you three years ago. I love you now. I'll always—'

Cass didn't get a chance to finish as he dragged her into his arms and began to kiss her breathless. When he'd finished, she still couldn't speak because her heart was full.

'You'd better always love me,' he told her fiercely, 'because I won't let you go again.'

'I will,' Cass said with utter certainty.

'So, church or register office?'

'What?'

'I assumed you were practising for our wedding.'

There was a teasing note in his voice, but underneath he was deadly serious.

'Shouldn't we live together for a while?'

'Why?'

It was a good question.

He followed it with, 'Are you certain you love me, Cass?'

She nodded but it was hardly necessary. Now there was no need to hide her feelings, there was love in every look she gave him.

'Let's make the commitment, then,' he added quietly.

He was asking her to put her trust in him, to accept the strength of his love and have faith in her own. It was the way people used to do it. They met, fell in love and married, expecting ups and downs but accepting they would stay together for ever.

'Yes, let's,' Cass agreed softly in return.

They did so, one short month later. It was a modest church affair. In some ways it wasn't the happiest day of Cass's life because too many memories of that other wedding intruded, and, despite everything, Cass still grieved for her little sister and a life cut dramatically short.

But one moment would remain with her. It was the defining moment after they'd exchanged vows and he'd slipped the ring on her finger and they'd looked at each other. No one else saw it, just them. It was there, however.

The promise of love everlasting in their eyes.

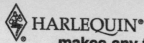

Double your pleasure—
with this collection containing two full-length

Harlequin Romance®

novels

New York Times bestselling author

DEBBIE MACOMBER

delivers

RAINY DAY KISSES

While Susannah Simmons struggles up the corporate
ladder, her neighbor Nate Townsend stays home baking
cookies and flying kites. She resents the way he questions
her values—and the way he messes up her five-year plan
when she falls in love with him!

PLUS

THE BRIDE PRICE

a brand-new novel by reader favorite

DAY LECLAIRE

On sale July 2001

HARLEQUIN®

Makes any time special ®

HARLEQUIN *Presents*
Passion™

Looking for stories that **sizzle**?

Wanting a read that has a little extra **spice**?

Harlequin Presents® is thrilled to bring you romances that turn up the **heat**!

Every other month there'll be a
PRESENTS PASSION™
book by one of your favorite authors.

Don't miss
THE ARABIAN MISTRESS
by **Lynne Graham**
On-sale June 2001, Harlequin Presents® #2182

and look out for
THE HOT-BLOODED GROOM
by **Emma Darcy**
On-sale August 2001, Harlequin Presents® #2195

Pick up a **PRESENTS PASSION**™ novel—
where **seduction** is guaranteed!

Available wherever Harlequin books are sold.

HARLEQUIN®
Makes any time special ®

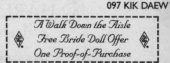

Harlequin invites you to walk down the aisle...

To honor our year long celebration of weddings, we are offering an exciting opportunity for you to own the Harlequin Bride Doll. Handcrafted in fine bisque porcelain, the wedding doll is dressed for her wedding day in a cream satin gown accented by lace trim. She carries an exquisite traditional bridal bouquet and wears a cathedral-length dotted Swiss veil. Embroidered flowers cascade down her lace overskirt to the scalloped hemline; underneath all is a multi-layered crinoline.

Join us in our celebration of weddings by sending away for your own Harlequin Bride Doll. This doll regularly retails for $74.95 U.S./approx. $108.68 CDN. One doll per household. Requests must be received no later than December 31, 2001. Offer good while quantities of gifts last. Please allow 6-8 weeks for delivery. Offer good in the U.S. and Canada only. Become part of this exciting offer!

**Simply complete the order form and mail to:
"A Walk Down the Aisle"**

<u>IN U.S.A</u>
P.O. Box 9057
3010 Walden Ave.
Buffalo, NY 14269-9057

<u>IN CANADA</u>
P.O. Box 622
Fort Erie, Ontario
L2A 5X3

Enclosed are eight (8) proofs of purchase found in the last pages of every specially marked Harlequin series book and $3.75 check or money order (for postage and handling). Please send my Harlequin Bride Doll to:

_____
Name (PLEASE PRINT)

_____
Address   Apt. #

_____
City   State/Prov.   Zip/Postal Code

_____
Account # (if applicable)   **097 KIK DAEW**

HARLEQUIN®
Makes any time special ®

Visit us at www.eHarlequin.com

*A Walk Down the Aisle
Free Bride Doll Offer
One Proof-of-Purchase*

PHWDAPOPR2